Date Due

FACULTY		OCT 8
FEB 21	JUN 25 1984
FEB	JUL 16 1984
JUL 9 1973	
JUN 24 1974	
JUL 7 1974	
APR 30 1975	

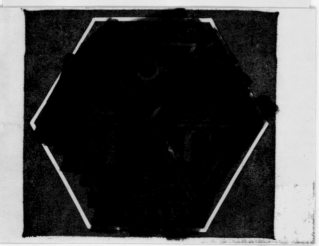

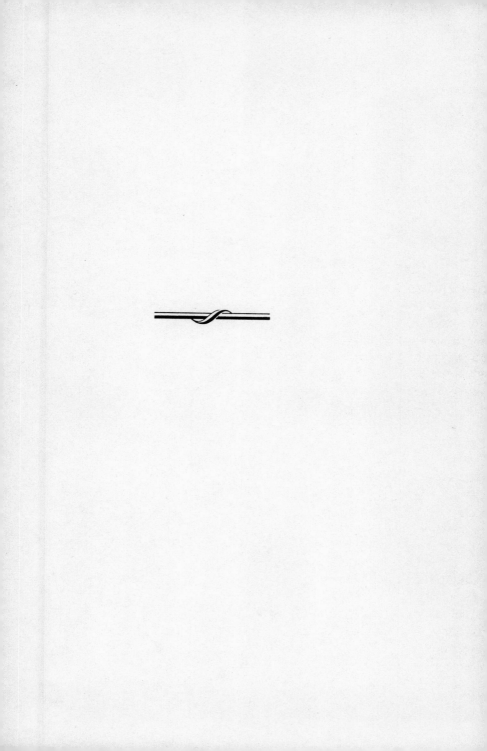

SHADES
OF
DIFFERENCE

Constance Bartusis

ST. MARTIN'S PRESS, NEW YORK

To
Joseph

Contents

SHADES OF DIFFERENCE

JAKE

It was a golden day in Mansfield. An aged September sun, no longer the gentle guardian of spring, beat harshly on her charges. But to Greg Davis, who was so sure of himself and satisfied with the way things were going, it was all delicious. The wide scorched lawns were like mammoth straw welcome mats; the dried orange leaves still holding out on the trees hissed and rustled.

Greg took his time walking Virginia home from school. His moist hand held her moist hand as he silently went over the scores he had already made—a good start in school, first-string basketball, the part-time job. Today he would spend his first evening as a junior counselor at the recreation center. There were worse jobs a guy could have—and the extra money would be nice. He had one of the prettiest girls in class, too, he thought as he surveyed again her golden skin, her honey hair, the three beauty spots that marked a triangle on her rose cheek. Things turned out all right if you plugged as you were supposed to, despite the stories he heard from Dad.

From the front porch of her home, Virginia's mother leaned out and tugged her blouse away from her body as she squinted at the two black figures cut out against the golden

3

sky. They looked as if they weren't moving at all, she thought irritably. All that trouble to arrange for an earlier dinner so that they could be at Mrs. Bryce's at six. But Virginia had to dawdle on the street with . . . that boy. She sighed and returned to the air-conditioned comfort of the house.

It was hot and they had walked silently, but Virginia felt the irritation setting in. "I must date the busiest boy in the whole school," she snapped.

"What did you say?" said Greg.

"I said, I must date the busiest boy in the whole school."

"What's the matter?"

"You have practice on Mondays and Thursdays, and now you have a job. I don't know what you're going to do when the season starts and you have to practice every day. Why do you have to work on Fridays?"

"To keep you in cokes and movies."

"Oh, you!"

Greg smiled. He knew he could tease old Ginny with impunity. She was smart and a good sport and generous with her own big allowance. "You have me on Saturdays, you know."

"Big deal."

"I told you I'd be over after work, didn't I?"

"And what time will that be?"

"About nine thirty."

"Well, it's too late to go out. But if you hurry maybe we can catch some of the kids at Rex's."

"The kids? Who wants to see the kids?" They were in the privacy of Virginia's porch now and Greg pulled her close. "I can think of better things to do than chase after people." The girl lowered her eyes with the practiced modesty of a teenage coquette.

"Virginia!" her mother called shrilly from behind the screen door.

Greg broke away. "Hello, Mrs. Ashburn. Hot, isn't it?"

"Virginia . . . Oh . . . Hello, Greg. Yes . . . it is. Virginia,

4

dear, Mrs. Bryce wants us to come over for a special meeting tonight. I told her we could make it by six. What took you so long? Never mind. Just come in quickly and eat." It seemed as if she said it all in one breath and disappeared.

"She knows I always get home at four," Virginia grumbled. "But when Mag the Hag calls, Mother really jumps. Big Friday night. All the girls will be out with their steadies but I have to spend it with the Burnside Physic League."

Greg never failed to smile at Virginia's pet name for the Civic League. They were a bunch of yo-yo's all right. He had seen them in action when they were meeting at Virginia's house and she had invited him over for laughs. They had spent the whole night quibbling over the name of the organization—Mag wanted to change it to the Burnside "Cultural" League. It sounded more . . . true to the purpose of the League, she had said. They did raise a lot of money for the cultural center. It sounded more . . . specific. And all the ladies agreed with her.

But that was precisely the trouble, thought the men. "Well, now," skinny old John McGinnis of McGinnis' drugstore drawled on recognition by the chair, "considering that the League has committees like the Citizens' Corps for Neighborhood Beauty, and the Citizens' Deportment Council, it looks to me like Mrs. Bryce's suggestion narrows the picture a bit." McGinnis sat back puffing his pipe and was reassured by a nod and a wink from fat Toddy Johnson, father of the basketball team's fat student manager.

"I agree with John," Toddy said. "The League was established to make Burnside the leading community in the city. And as we look back on our past achievements"—Toddy stood up, leaned back belly out, and stuck his thumbs under his lapels—"we see that the Burnside Civic League has delved into the areas of sanitation, finance, and even personal conduct, so that the name 'Burnside *Cultural* League' would not tell the whole story." Toddy ended on a loud note and plopped down with an air of conclusiveness, satisfied by the shifting and murmuring of the men.

5

It was Virginia's mother who had made the final attempt to rally the Bryce forces. "But beautifying comes under the idea of culture," she said. More murmuring. But it was too late. The motion to change the name was defeated; "Burnside Civic League" it remained. The League doubled their annual variety events to two and the meeting adjourned.

"I can't blame you for not wanting to be there," Greg said. "What do you suppose she wants?"

"Oh . . . I guess it's about the variety show next month. But I don't see why I have to be there. I've been practicing every day and I have the staging all worked out." Virginia was dancing a selection from *Giselle*. "I guess Mom just wants a bigger army."

"Should I still come over then?"

"Sure. I'll bet Biddy Bryce goes to bed at nine o'clock."

"Well, I'll see you then. I'd better hurry." Greg kissed her on the cheek and, hot as it was, ran the few blocks toward home. There was still supper to eat and a bus to catch.

———✦———

The *colored section*, he thought to himself as he peered out the bus window at the landmarks along Cole Avenue. He had been through Cole before but today the sights along its main artery came alive. In the months to come it would be a second home. He was amused; it was just as you'd picture it: shingles with names like "Washington" and "Lincoln" dotted its professional section; store-front churches, pawnshops, bars and outdoor markets spotted its long, shabby commercial stretch; people swarmed like flies along the street— shapely brown girls in bright, snug clothes, sharpies in T-shirts and hats, withered little brown men in shiny suits, fat mama's with shopping bags, little girls with woolly braids.

"Fisher Street!" Greg was shaken from his trance. He stumbled down to the front of the bus and peered out at the left side of the street. A playground down the block. A ball

6

field in back of it. That must be it. The bus came to a stop, and with a hiss of air the folding doors opened and Greg jumped down. It was even hotter here in the city, and he at once missed the cool breeze from the open bus window.

As he crossed the avenue he noticed a vacant building with smeared windows and a sign that said AVAILABLE FOR RENT. Next to that was Basil's Confectionery. Greg was startled by the unexpected appearance of a white girl. She was a real looker, too, he thought as he studied her long, slender figure. She was backing out against the screen door of Basil's, her arms filled with bundles. The girl swung around, and Greg caught a glimpse of slanted bright blue eyes under high arching brows. Then she walked briskly ahead of him, her silky yellow hair tossing with each quick step.

To his surprise she turned at the same grimy red brick building to which he was heading, followed a path alongside the playground, and disappeared into a back entrance. He stopped, then went in through the front door and up a small flight of stairs. The clock above a trophy case said 5:24. To the left of the landing was a kitchen; to the right of it was an office. A gangly white boy sat on the edge of a desk talking to a stocky Negro man with close-shaved hair.

"Pardon me," said Greg as he appeared at the doorway. "I'm looking for Mr. Waters."

"That's me." The Negro grinned, rose and extended his hand. He had a knotty set of muscles that looked like a gnarled tree. "Tom Davis' boy?"

"Yes . . . Hello. How did you know it was . . . who I am?"

"Ah, you look like your daddy," the man said. Greg's father was a social worker and his connections had helped Greg to get the job. "This is Dick Roper, whose place you're taking," Doc Waters went on as he slapped the boy's shoulder.

The boy's shook hands and mumbled how-do-you-do's.

"Dick here said he'd stay on for a half hour and show you

7

around. Too bad you didn't get here a couple of minutes earlier. Our gal Mitzi went out for some cokes and she could have brought you something, too."

"That's all right. Water will be fine."

"Well, take your time. The suppertime crowd isn't here yet. I have some reports to get out, so I'm gonna get with it."

"First you'll have to change clothes," said Dick. A door leading off to the right of the office said STAFF LOUNGE. It was a large room partitioned into three sections by sliding bamboo screens, and behind one of them was a small slice of room containing a clothes rack and a wooden chair. Greg put on his sand-colored pants, T-shirt and tennis shoes.

"Here," said Dick. "You might as well take these now." It was a chain with three keys on it. "Big one's for this equipment locker. Want to see what's in it?" It was filled with the usual equipment—basketballs, volley balls, softballs, bats, tennis racquets and tennis balls, badminton racquets and shuttlecocks, ping-pong paddles, games, a first-aid kit and some unfamiliar items. "There's some stuff down in the game room, too," Dick went on. "Mostly art supplies. Every night before closing we take a tally"—he pointed to a check list taped on the inside of the locker door—"and whoever does it marks a zero for what's missing and signs his initials. You'll see. How many nights are you working here?"

"Tuesday, Friday and every other Saturday nine till five."

They walked to the small kitchenette. A short brown-haired woman sat at the table eating an omelet and opposite her was the blonde girl Greg had seen outside. "La-dies," said Dick, "this is our new counselor, Greg Davis. Greg, this is Miss MacCartney and Mitzi Stevens. Mac's the girls' coach and Mitzi's a counselor like us."

"We're glad to have you here, Greg," the blonde girl said in a deep smooth voice.

"Sure, we'll be glad to trade Dick for you any day," said Mac.

Dick punched her in the arm. "I'll make sure I come

8

around to plague you once in a while. Oh—I have a better idea. I'll tell Lester Peterson to come around and keep you busy." Both of the women groaned. "Come on, Greg. Let's get away from these dames."

They looked over the basement facilities and came back upstairs to go outside. "My Dad says you're starting college," Greg said to Dick.

"That's right. I have to be there Monday."

"Mansfield?"

"No. State. That's why I have to quit work." The State University was about a hundred miles away from Mansfield. "Mitzi says it's not a good idea to work your first year in college anyway."

"She's in college already?"

"Yes."

"Then she's older."

Dick looked at Greg and smiled. "Almost twenty-one, I guess. She's a senior already. Besides, she's engaged. She went to State for two years and met this . . . this guy up there. He's in law school." The boy turned to Greg with a curious look of indecision. "Then she transferred to Mansfield. Said she wanted to save money."

"When does she work?"

"Every night except Tuesdays and Thursdays. She's our unofficial secretary in a way. Here's the basketball court; over there's the tennis court," Dick said, pointing. Only the basketball court was paved, a conspicuous concrete strip on the dusty ground, and a little Negro boy raced furiously around it on a homemade scooter, swirling behind him a gritty cloud of sand.

They were near the pool now, and Greg noted that its bottom was bare and rough. Behind it and the playground stretched a bumpy dirt ballfield. The bleachers that lined just one side of the field were dried out and rotten, and there was no scoreboard.

"Kind of small, considering all the kids who must live around here, isn't it?" said Greg.

9

Dick nodded. "Doc's been complaining about that for years, but nobody's doing anything about it. Well, I have to be going pretty soon."

"Where do you live?"

"Hampton."

"Did you graduate from Hampton High?"

"Uh-huh."

"Do you know the Murdocks? Kathy Murdock?"

"Oh, yeah. She likes to swim. She's always at the pool."

"She's my cousin."

"She's cute. Well . . . I know you'll like it here, Greg. The kids are pretty nice and Doc's a good guy to work for. He's tough and he'll always back you up when you have trouble. Is there anything you want to know?"

"Mmm . . . no. I think I have a pretty good idea of what to do."

"It's really easy. You'll catch on quick."

"If you have to leave, I don't want to hold you up."

"My bus will be coming."

"Nice meeting you, Dick. And thanks again for sticking around."

"That's all right. Me and Mitzi did some cleaning and organizing for Doc. Hope I see you around."

" 'By, Dick and good luck in school."

Greg found a shady spot by the wall near the street and studied the few kids who had trickled into the park. At the side entrance that led to the game room were three boys. One of them, a short Negro with a Tyrolean hat, bobbed up and down and snapped his fingers and wobbled his head as he sang to himself. Colored guys were sure funny sometimes, Greg thought to himself. Who else could dance around and wear a felt hat on such a hot day? One of his companions was a sleepy-looking white boy with dirty-blond hair and acne who looked too tired to move. The third was a neat, fine-featured Negro with a thin mustache who stood tall, bored and unaffected by the sun's raging.

In a short time the center was crowded. Three Negro girls

in bright summer play clothes swaggered into the park. One of them was short and shapely with yellow slacks slung low over her hips and a short blouse that just brushed her navel. A second was a tall graceful girl with a long black pony tail who looked as cool as lime sherbet in chartreuse slacks and a jersey that matched. Their friend was lumps of chocolate fat with orange shorts and a painfully stretched halter and she smiled a pleasant, wide-toothed grin. They formed a private circle near the flagpole and took their conversation very seriously.

"Sally, Ba-BY!" The shriek from the dancing Negro boy rang across the court startling everybody, and the girl in yellow slacks smacked her lips with disapproval as she turned her head away. In a short time they were approached by a homely girl with stiff straight hair and glasses but seeing her, they walked away and resettled near Greg.

Two little Negro boys, oblivious to the deadening heat, raced wildly after a woolly-haired third with enormous eyes who held a volley ball as he dodged and darted about like a mouse. He wriggled out of the grasp of his larger foes over and over again and between gasps for breath laughed a machine gun ha-ha-ha. Every once in a while one of the bigger boys would halt and holler "Alphonse! When I catch you, I'm gon' beat you!"

Then Greg heard one of the girls drawl a sugary "Hi Jake, honey," and he turned to see a tall, shirtless Negro boy standing at the entrance. The little bug-eyed boy with the volley ball ran up, tossed the visitor his booty and screamed a breathless "Here, Jake!" The white boy leaning against the doorway showed his first sign of life by whining a falsetto "Mah man. . . ." Jake seemed to be looking for someone. For a long time he peered around the park through bright black eyes, one long-fingered hand still clutching the volley ball at his hip. He turned to the fat girl in orange, "Where's your brother?"—she shrugged her shoulders; then to the three boys, "Seen Dumbo?" The dancer opened his eyes wide, rolled his lip under in a great sad pout and slowly shook his

11

head. Jake flipped the volley ball back to Alphonse and went inside, the three boys following him. The last of them to enter was the sleepy white boy who merely rolled around the doorway.

Greg heard a clock chime six from some distant church. It was time for him to go in.

He found Doc Waters in the gym tying up a volley ball net. "Who's playing tonight?" he asked.

"A ladies' club from around here," Doc answered. "Sometimes they do exercises with Mac, sometimes they play volley ball. You know the bit—a night out for mammy."

"Dick mentioned that there's a gym schedule."

"Well, we have a lot of people around here who want to use the facilities, so we have to keep some order. The schedule's up on the gym door. When we're setting up—like now—the kids can come in if they have gym shoes. Or if they take their street shoes off like Jake over there." Greg turned and saw the boy near the center line, getting set for a long shot.

"I came to ask you where I should start."

"Let's see. Mitzi's down in the game room so you might as well station yourself outside in the park. Get the kids what they want. See they don't fight. Keep your eye on everything. Play some of their games."

"Sounds easy enough."

"You'll be busier than you think." Doc looped the rope in a circle and gave the knot a firm tug. Then he looked up and frowned. "On your way out, *there's* something for you to do." Greg turned and saw the three boys from outside talking to Jake. "Those tough guys have their shoes on again. Come draggin' themselves in here with cleats on their shoes and mess up the floor. Chase 'em off. Might as well get acquainted with our local celebrities."

Greg walked over to the group reluctantly. "Uh . . . pardon me," he said. But the boys didn't seem to hear. "Excuse me," Greg said a little louder. "You . . . uh . . . have your shoes on."

12

The short boy bowed dramatically, stared at his feet and swooped up again with widened eyes. "So I do! Can you imagine that? I got my SHOOOES on!"

Greg felt himself getting hot and hoped his face hadn't turned red. He pretended to ignore the remarks and continued. "You're not allowed on the gym floor with hard-soled shoes." Then he began to feel brave. "I'm sorry. But you'll have to go on the side."

The boy with the hat put his hand on his hip and stared with mock stupefaction. The tall, slick-looking Negro looked out above Greg's head as though Greg weren't even there. The white boy gave him a dirty look. After what seemed an endless time the three shared a sneer and slowly left the floor. Punks, thought Greg. He was angry that he had had to get involved with them and he could hardly wait to get out of the gym. He turned toward the exit furthest from where they were sitting and walked away with a sense of business.

"Don't worry, chief. They always do that," came a voice from behind him. He knew it was the boy named Jake so he didn't bother to turn around.

Outside it went pretty much the same as evenings Greg had spent as a child at the Burnside center. A few children were in the building with checkers, parcheesi and crafts, but most of them preferred the breezy onslaughts of cool air that met them as they ran and jumped and climbed. The small ones were informally isolated near the swings and climbing bars; adolescents formed large teams at the volley ball court where they jumped and stretched and clandestinely enjoyed teamwork with the opposite sex. There were the lost and out of place: two mature, sultry girls leaned under the sliding board, smoking and flirting with a muscular Negro boy. Across the nearly empty end of the playground some young boys had transformed the amorphous corner into a small softball diamond, and in the main ballfield two teams of grown young men played a serious game of football.

Memory of his childhood days guided Greg at his duties.

13

He instinctively scolded tiny children who raced too close to the swings or came down the slide backwards or fought and tumbled on the ground. He joined in one volley ball game and his team won. When the boys playing softball broke their own bat, he got them the center's with CRC written in red nail polish on the tape. Everyone was friendly and cooperative. At least four times, small groups of saucer-eyed children came up and sang, "What's you na-ame?" and a couple of the older boys asked, "What happened to Dick?"

As Greg watched the boys playing football, someone said, "Need any help?" He turned around. There was Mitzi.

"No, everything's under control. But . . . but do you have to go inside right away?" He looked at her blue eyes and thought how pretty she was.

"The craft room closes at a quarter after eight, so I'll have to start cleaning up soon." She watched the game for a few minutes, then turned to Greg again. "Are you in high school?"

Greg sulked. "Does it show that much?"

"No," Mitzi laughed. "Doc mentioned it. Where do you go?"

"Burnside Heights. I'm a junior."

"Oh, really?" She looked surprised. "Do you know Harry Garsky?"

"Garsky? Mr. Garsky? He's my P.O.D. . . . my Problems of Democracy teacher."

"My uncle."

"Yeah?"

"Uh-huh."

"Small world, I like him. He's a good teacher and the assistant sponsor of the History Club . . . of which I'm president—AHEM!"

Mitzi smiled. "Good for you."

"I'll mention that I met you next time I talk to him."

Mitzi spent a few minutes talking with Greg about the kids who came to the park and about what problems to expect. She then returned to the game room.

14

Before Greg realized how fast the time was passing, it had become harder to see and the crowd had dwindled. Everywhere competition had given way to horseplay—only two girls were volleying now and the softball game had deteriorated to a three-way game of catch. In the relative quiet Greg heard the clock chime again eight times. He saw Doc taking down the swings and walked over.

"Doesn't look like there's too much for me to do now," he said. "Can I help you with something?"

"No, but check the equipment locker and gather up the balls. Might as well learn what that's all about. Oh . . . and take down the volley ball net in the gym. Mac can't untie my knots."

There were one volley ball and one basketball missing. When he went outside late dusk had given way to night and Greg could barely distinguish the black forms of the volleyball players from the blue-black night. One down, he thought as he passed them by. The problem of the missing basketball was solved, too. In the court two boys were randomly shooting and catching rebounds. A Tyrolean hat hanging on a post told him who one of the boys was. He peered through the darkness, the other was the white boy. The tall mustached Negro was sitting quite still on one of the benches, his legs crossed, his arms resting on the back of the seat.

What luck, Greg thought, as he forced himself to walk towards the court. The street light just outside the playground illuminated the keyhole. Through the darkness someone whined, "Aw man, you gonna take the ball from us?"

"No," said Greg. "The park doesn't close till eight-thirty. I'm . . . uh . . . just checking up on things. Were you having a game?"

"No, man," squealed the short boy. "We just messin' around. Just messin' around." He dribbled the ball a few times and flipped it to the boy on the bench. "Hey, Jim Dandy. Wanna' have a game? We need another head."

No sound. The boy on the bench just shook his head slowly.

"What you good for anyway?" the short boy hollered to his friend. Then to Greg, "Jim Dandy never wants to get messed up." He went to retrieve the ball and Greg looked after him, a little confused. He hadn't meant to imply that he wanted to join them . . . but suddenly the ball bounced at him. Well, why not? he thought. There was nothing much for him to do at work and he might as well make peace with these guys if they hung around the place a lot. Now that there were three having a free-for-all, two boys would guard the one who had the ball. The short colored boy, whose name was Lester, was fast and tricky and sunk all kinds of shots. For a while they had a fast session.

At one point Greg leaped up to catch a rebound. Then he gasped out loud. The air rushed from his lungs, the ball rolled from his fingertips. The boys had crashed into his stomach. "Foul!" he hollered. But the boys were on the other side of the keyhole. The white boy was waving the ball and ducking while Lester jumped and kicked and swatted and shrieked, "Haw! Haw!" "Cut it out. Cut it out, man," the white boy whined.

Then somehow Lester grabbed the ball and began dribbling low and fast while the white boy lazily flapped his thin arms and legs through the air. Greg hesitated but finally went over. He swung around in front of Lester and began swatting at the ball. One low slap connected hard, the ball punched the cyclone fence and dropped behind a bench. Lester moaned. The two boys didn't seem to care so Greg retrieved the ball and dribbled toward the basket, planning to make a last shot and leave. He was in the clear . . . then he screamed out. Someone had kicked him in the shin. He tried to hide his pain but he had to suck in breath and moan. Fear froze his body and emptied out his mind as he dumbly watched the ball roll and roll until it went under a bench and disappeared. Then voices brought him back to attention and he stiffened for a fight.

16

Lester was hollering. "You dumb cracker! You step all over the chief's nice white shoes!"

"Aw, man. . . ."

"Shoot! You just clumsy, Whitey!"

Greg stood there shaking. No one else was outside with them. He hobbled over to the bench to get the ball, then waited confused and afraid in the safety and privacy of the darkness. Again, they seemed to have forgotten him. Apes, he thought.

The white boy was on the other side of the court scraping imaginary mud off his shoes and talking to "Jim Dandy." Lester was still in the keyhole doing some weird dance on the foul line. He swung his arms backwards in wide circles while he shuffled back on his left foot and bounced his right toe behind it. Through the thick darkness came the soft drone of a familiar Ray Charles song:

I'm gonna drown in my own tears,
Gonna drown in my own tears. . . .

Greg couldn't wait to get inside the building. He wanted to run but was afraid to. Running could invite a chase. He stared frozen and helpless at the boys, trying to read what they might do. After a while he decided he could gain composure by taking a couple of long shots and exit cool. He steadied himself near the center line and studied the basket with deliberate nonchalance. The stretching felt good and relaxed him. One ball bounced off the rim and arched right back into his outstretched arms. He caught it, flexed his knees and pushed his arms up again. This time the ball, released abortively, just dropped. Greg buckled and clutched himself. He stared at the banking board, there was a numbness in his neck. The boys had rammed him hard from both sides and Lester's palm was slicing down again. He trembled and stumbled forward, ready to fall.

Then there was someone else in the street lamp's cone of light and Greg heard, "Aw . . . that's enough, monkeys!" It was the boy named Jake. Now his long fingers were around the necks of Lester and Whitey and he was shaking them.

"Aaagh! Leggo-Jake-you're killing-me!" Lester yelled.

And Jake, partly scolding, partly pleading, wailed, "What's the matter with you apes?" He shoved them away.

"Aw, man, we just havin' a little game with the chief," said Whitey.

Lester was rubbing his neck and rolling his head and hissing. "Shoot, Jake, that hurt! Oo-oo-oo! My neck!"

"G'wan," Jake droned. "Why don't you do something healthy like tourist jiving?"

"Comin' Jake?"

"I guess so."

Lester kicked, swirled and twisted his way over to his hat. Greg wondered if he'd ever leave. Finally he snatched the hat, flicked its brush and carefully arranged it on his head. Then he began tucking his T-shirt in his slacks.

"Shake it, man!" Jake hollered. "The boy gotta close up."

Lester strutted back to his friends, slapping down his heels to the upbeat of the same song:

Baby, I fe-el so-o blue,
Yeah, I fe-el so-o blue. . . .

At the keyhole he finished the song with great showmanship while his three friends waited patiently.

Greg stood by in the dark, still dazed, still confused, but fascinated. Hugging the basketball, he took a last look around the park. He'd shower and dress and get out of this hole, he thought bitterly. Soon he would be with Virginia, and if she asked him anything, he'd tell her what animals the people down here really were and that everything people said about them was probably true.

———

From where Greg sat on the gym floor, Rich Wallace, captain of the Burnside varsity, really looked mean. He stood with his left foot up on the bench and leaning over,

18

looked down at the eighteen boys who sat on the floor. Greg was sitting right in front, practically beneath Rich's chin, and from that angle it looked even bigger than it actually was. Rich's skin was damp with sweat and rosy from the workout they had just had. He spoke in clipped syllables through tight thin lips that never smiled and the muscles in his neck throbbed as he spoke. His grey eyes ran parallel to straight bushy brows and his thick brown hair, now wet and wild, reached over his forehead like talons. As Virginia had so aptly put it, he was handsome in a brutish way.

Even though it was only the beginning of October, the Burnside Bats were already following a slow-paced practice season. "We've got a pretty good exhibition schedule this year," Rich was saying. "A game on the twenty-fourth with Marlow, the northern regional champs. That's only three and a half weeks away, so you drips better get in shape. We don't want to look sick and like I said, they were only a couple of steps away from state champs." The gym was as quiet as a church. "Day before Hallowe'en we go to Bedford. That's a little Blacktown about seventy miles from here. McKing says they're tough this year. Says they're fast. So us lead seats better pep it up, because we're not gonna let a bunch of black boys beat us. It's a good trip too. If you come in your own car you can cruise around the town after the game and have some kicks. Most of you guys wouldn't remember, but two years ago, when Carl and Danny and I were sophomores, we played them. Good time, wasn't it?" The two boys nodded silently at the back of the group.

"Season starts November twentieth with Hampton High, but we'll worry about that later. Okay. We should go for city champs again and man, we'd better take it." Rich wrapped up his remarks about scheduling and began assessing the first team out loud. "Davis looks like he's in good shape, so's Carl. But Klingle and Hoffman, here. You blubber tanks. Stop eating so much strudel and schnitzel. You both looked tired today from dragging those pots around." Greg glanced around and grinned at seeing the faces of the new team-

19

mates. They were looking at each other with confusion in their eyes. "Another thing, Hoffman," Rich went on, "you'd better stop hanging around with Mary Lou so late every night."

"Hey, Rich!" Danny Hoffman hollered indignantly, and Rich Wallace laughed.

Greg was used to Wallace's mouthing off by now but remembered how many times he was tempted to have it out with him. He wondered if any of the new boys, looking so timid and dumb, felt that way. No, he concluded; they were still too cowed by it all.

But one of them, a promising sophomore guard named Scrappy Hull, thought he'd join the capping. Cupping his hand over his mouth, he hollered good-naturedly, "And try to stop Mona from chasing Carl!" Mona was Rich's sister. Most of the boys smiled. Rich feigned indifference; then a sudden cutting obscenity he aimed at Sparky wiped the smiles off the faces and stunned the group into a sad, fearful somberness. Greg reddened and felt a little sick. No doubt about it; Rich could really be mean.

"What are you planning to do about that job, Davis?" The question broke the awkward lull that hung over the team and caught Greg by surprise.

"Huh? What do you mean?"

"The job. The job. The league games are on Friday, you know that. So are some of the exhibition games. And we're going to be practicing full time after a while. How are you gonna do it?"

"Oh, I'll just switch days with this girl at work. I already talked to. . . ."

"I don't care what you do. Just make sure you don't come to the games dragging your end." The boys tittered.

"Okay, sad sacks. Let's get out of here." Rich Wallace spun around and walked away.

As Greg walked back to the locker room he was amused by the muttering of the scrubs. "That Wallace sure is funny, huh?" said one.

"Are you crazy? I'd hate to get on his wrong side," said another.

"Yeah. He sounds bad."

———⚯———

When Greg entered the office the following evening, Mitzi was at the desk doing some clerical work. As she looked up, he grinned self-consciously. "How are you today, Greg?"

"Not bad." He leaned over the desk. "What are you doing?"

"End of the month expense report." She was wearing cologne.

"Mmm. That smells nice."

"Thank you," Mitzi said sweetly.

It was just one of those quiet boy-girl things—she was safely engaged—a mutual appreciation. "Well . . . to the salt mines," said Greg and went into the staff room to change.

He found Doc Waters unlocking the gym door. "What's going on tonight?" he asked.

"The Blackhawks are practicing," Doc answered, pushing open the door and jamming down the stop with his foot. "The Nightowls practiced yesterday and the Amigos come tomorrow. Take a look at the schedule, boy." Doc walked to the other end of the gym and his voice trailed off. "Gotta get some air in here." He walked to the window with a pole. "Hey Greg?"

"Yes?"

"Go down and open the locker room. Here!" He hurled a bunch of keys high into the air. "Bring up anything that's left down there."

"Right." Greg went downstairs and after some trial and error, found the key that clicked the door open. He groped for a light switch, walked in and began searching.

Thumping on the stairs interrupted his inspection. One of the boys Greg had encountered on his first night—the civilized one, appeared in the doorway with a satchel. He strode

21

into the room with long, brisk steps, taking no note of Greg. Greg, not sure whether he had been seen, said "Hi" to play safe.

"Oh . . ." Jake looked up, surprised. "Hi."

"Uh . . . you play for the Blackhawks?"

"Yeah."

"What time's practice?"

"Six. Six thirty."

"You're . . . uh . . . early."

"Yeah . . . well . . . by the time I get home from school and get something to eat, I have an hour, hour and a half to kill. So I just come right on down here. Have the gym to my-self."

"You go to Cole High School?"

"Yeah."

Seems friendly enough, thought Greg. "Uh . . . doesn't Cole have a basketball team?"

"Yeah," Jake answered with a curt matter-of-factness, feel-ing a bit resentful of Greg's queries. He looked at Greg boldly and curiously for a few moments, as though sizing him up. Then, as though changing his mind about some-thing, explained, "But Cole ain't got much of a team. And I ain't no cheerleader, see? I just want a good game, that's all. You dig it?"

"Y-yes. It's not such a small school, though."

"No. Not specially. But the kids ain't interested in that rah-rah stuff. And the big boys and the good ballplayers—like Les Peterson, f'rinstance—don't stay in school long enough to make good on varsity."

"Who?" Greg couldn't think of any common acquaint-ances and was surprised at the mention of a name.

"Lester. You know. The dancing fool. With the hat . . . ?"

"Oh, yes," Greg groaned.

"Now old Les is a real fine ballplayer for his size. He has speed. Shine. He woulda been in my class, but he quit school." Jake turned to leave for practice.

"Uh . . . does Lester play for the Blackhawks, too?" Greg

asked quickly. He certainly wanted to know when to expect that character around again.

"Shoot!" Jake hissed. "My man Les? Not him. You have to be around to practice on Saturday mornings, man. Les ain't up till noon or later. He's too tired from hanging around the poolroom Friday, or going to a dance, or tourist jivin' till all hours."

"Tourist jiving?"

"Yeah."

"What's that?"

"Aw, come on, baby."

Greg reddened and thought hard.

"Tourin'. You know?" Jake prompted. "Tourin' Darktown?"

Greg just shook his head.

"You a white boy and you don't know what tourin' Darktown is? Tsk! Tsk! Tsk!" Jake scolded playfully. Then he threw back his head and laughed.

Greg was confused and angry. Punk, he thought.

And Jake didn't let up. "You're a nice boy."

"I'll see you around," Greg said coldly and turned away.

"Hey!"

Greg turned and looked at him challengingly.

"Ain't no sense gettin' mad. You gonna be workin' around here, you gonna be seein' a lot of me."

"Forget it."

"You like basketball?"

"Yeah," Greg said casually, not wanting to sound too friendly. "I play a little myself."

Jake put one foot up on a bench and folded his arms over his thigh. "Then you probably know Telly Howard."

"Sure." Any basketball fan knew about Howard. He was the Negro forward from Cole who had been signed up by the Eagles a couple of years ago with a big bonus.

"Telly used to play right here for the Blackhawks before he was signed up by the Eagles," Jake went on.

"Oh. I didn't know that."

23

"Hey. How about that championship game last year?" Jake rambled on. Greg remembered it well. He had won five dollars from Frank Klinglehaus in a bet on it.

". . . made me a five spot on that game"—Jake echoed his thoughts, and Greg laughed and explained the coincidence. "He-ey," Jake droned, "put it here." And the next thing he knew and the next thing Greg knew, the colored boy's hand was out to shake on it and they were both staring at it. Then Greg reached out quickly as though nothing was wrong and the hands circled once and withdrew.

"You know Telly personally?" asked Greg.

"Sort of. Almost everyone around here knows Telly. He was in my brother's class. They hung around together once in a while. Wasn't as smart as Danny; but that don't make no difference." Jake was suddenly somber. "Telly got kicked out of school 'cause he was so dumb, now he drives a Continental, comes in town lookin' sharp. He bought the old Lotus Hotel, fixed it up and sent his sick mother to a fancy old folks home. And Danny's in the army cause he didn't know what to do with hisself."

"Danny's your brother?"

"Yeah, Danny's my brother." And the colored boy's flecked brown eyes looked sad and troubled.

"Something the matter?" asked Greg.

It seemed an endless time till Jake answered. "You bet something's the matter, man. Danny was a real fine mechanic but he never could get a job. Danny Williams—you know him? Naw, you wouldn't know about Danny Williams —he's a soldier boy now," Jake snapped. Then for the longest time his body hung slouched over his knee and he stared at nothing.

These colored people, Greg thought, so emotional. Didn't he have any pride, to stand there and . . . blubber all his troubles to a perfect stranger? Everyone had problems. So Danny Williams was a soldier now. Big deal. So were a lot of other people. And as for not being able to get a job, what was so new about a manual laborer being unemployed with

24

automation around? These colored people. They still wanted to make a go of shining shoes.

He was irritated at having been trapped in the cellar with the boy for so long. Surely Doc would be wondering what he was doing. And Jake was just daydreaming now, like he didn't even know where he was. Greg had to say something before he left, though. "Is Telly your hero?" he asked lightly.

Jake's sudden glare told Greg that it was the wrong thing. "Nobody's my hero, baby," Jake said coldly and he stormed up to the gym.

Greg felt stunned and angry at having been entangled in the whole matter. He hadn't been nosy. He had always minded his own business. But this guy came along and dumped his problems on him like a bag of dirty laundry.

Danny Williams. Then Greg remembered why the name was so familiar. He remembered the incident of a year and a half ago because Dad had talked about it a lot. It was a big mess about job discrimination. Greg couldn't remember all the facts—he really hadn't paid too much attention at the time, but it was the first time union membership and job discrimination had been called to public attention in Mansfield. It had gotten a lot of publicity. It was the kind of thing that might have started real trouble with the wrong kind of people. Maybe Dad still had the clippings.

Greg slowly climbed the steps to the gym. When he arrived at the doorway he saw Jake Williams posed at the center line for a long shot. Jake Williams' brother, the subject of a discrimination scandal. Greg stared with the fascination of seeing a newspaper story come alive.

When he got home from work Greg made a sandwich and poured a glass of milk. His parents were in the living room reading the newspaper.

"Hey, Dad?"

"Yes?" Mr. Davis looked up from behind the sports section.

"Do you remember that newspaper story about a kid named Danny Williams a while back?"

"Williams? Oh, yes. That was only last summer."

"His brother comes to the park a lot."

"Oh, yes. There was a little brother."

"You know them?"

"Not really. When I was still with the welfare department they were on my case load."

"Well . . . what was that all about? That business two years ago?"

"Let's see. . . . Danny Williams had just graduated from high school as a shop student; he tried to get a job as mechanic with Teasdale Agricultural Machines, but no dice."

"Why?"

"The man doing the hiring told him he had to belong to the union."

"But we have right-to-work laws in this state."

"Yes. That was the first fishy thing. It turned out to be just plain passing the buck by everyone, because when Danny tried to join the union, he was denied membership."

"Why?"

"They said he was of undesirable character. They don't have to take everyone, and it wouldn't be good if they did. You can't discriminate on the basis of race or creed, but you can for reasons of character. And when people want to find reasons, they'll find them."

"Was anything wrong with Danny?"

"No. He had done well in school, and when the matter was brought into the open by civil rights people, witnesses testified to his good character. It was a mess. I'm sure both sides were sorry they had tried to get away with it but people on top don't like to go back on their word and they just left Williams smeared."

"But . . . but we never had anything like that in Mansfield before. People are prejudiced here . . . I guess . . . but we've never had discrimination in jobs and stuff like that."

"No, not officially. But plenty goes on, only it's kept quiet. Only Teasdale wasn't so lucky that time because colored people are starting to make noise."

"Why did the union lie like that? You'd think they're all workers . . ."

"There's been a shortage of jobs for the past couple of years. And people will use any excuse they can find to shut others out when it suits them. The Negroes are a ready-made answer to an awful lot of problems."

"Hmm. Maybe that's what prejudice is all about."

"Well . . . that's one of the things. You're awfully interested in this."

"Not really. I mean . . . of course I'm interested. I don't run around wearing blinders like you think I do. It's just that meeting Jake in person made me wonder what that was all about. He brought it up."

All his life Greg had heard that everyone had a free will, everyone had a chance to make good if he worked hard and did what he was told to do. Sometimes his father would talk about people who he said were really handicapped but Greg would think that he was just soft in the head from being a social worker too long. As ye sowed, so would ye reap.

Now Greg couldn't deny the sickening conclusion that someone had simply been victimized through no real fault of his own. No wonder Jake was so moody. He seemed like a pretty decent guy and perhaps he saw himself in a couple of years without a job, without the money to change things, without hope. No wonder he had gotten sore when Greg asked him if Telly was his hero. Telly's freakish success was one of those ironies that made you want to smash those fat, hot-dog eating fans who made him rich on whim while a straight guy like Danny couldn't work for a living. With a feeling of distaste, Greg had to admit two facts that he didn't like—that all men were not born equal, nor were they born free. In the future, he thought, he might not be so quick to judge people.

For a while he gazed absently at the back of his father's newspaper, then he called to his father again.

"What?" Mr. Davis said, looking up again.

"Did you ever hear of 'tourist jiving'?"

27

Mr. Davis smiled. "Where did you hear that?"

"Jake used the word but he wouldn't tell me what it meant."

"Can't you figure that one out? 'Jiving'—you know what that means—putting somebody on. And 'tourists,' well, they're white people who like to go snooping around through colored neighborhoods, looking for the seamier side of life and all kinds of loud behavior. Some get their kicks at the poverty itself."

"Oh," Greg uttered. He looked away, hoping his face wouldn't betray the fact that he had made a couple of such rides with Carl, Mona and Virginia during the summer.

"They expect a regular Porgy and Bess," Mr. Davis went on. "So on a lazy night with nothing else to do, some of the natives accommodate them with performances."

"I get it," said Greg, eager to drop the subject. "I'd better get upstairs and do some homework now." It had been enough for one night.

As early as 5:05 on Friday, Greg was already at his stop on Fisher Street. He had had a meeting after school and had come straight down to Cole with a stack of books, slacks and a jacket for the first senior high school dance of the year. There was still plenty of time to stop in Basil's for a sandwich.

Basil's was practically empty. One couple sat in a booth, a lone Negro boy sat way toward the back of the counter. The boy looked up and their eyes met. It was Jake Williams. His presence was so conspicuous that Greg felt obligated to join him.

"Hi." He slid onto the next stool.

"Hi," said Jake. "Man, that's a mighty load of books you got there, schoolboy."

"Yeah . . . well . . . I had to come straight to work after school today and didn't have time to drop them off at home."

"You must be a real bookworm."

"I don't always carry so many. It's just that I have a paper to start."

"Aw, man, I bet you always running around with lots of books. I bet your teachers just crazy about you."

Smart guy, huh? thought Greg. Well, he knew the type. Even a school like Burnside Heights had its share of goof-offs, the kids who were out of tune with school and never let you forget it. You just ignored them, that's all. Like Skippy Sullivan. Most of the kids at Burnside were frantic about things like getting through school and landing good jobs, but old Skippy didn't care about anything. He would probaby stay on soda jerking at McGinnis' drugstore where he had a part-time job. He clowned around and everybody laughed but he never really swayed anyone. Once in a while he got in trouble making noise in class and occasionally someone got caught helping him cheat but that was about all that happened.

He had just let this smart aleck Jake cut him up. Greg knew the score and this tough guy was in a bubble. He was from Cole and he was like all the rest—cut up, goof off, then cry because you couldn't get a job. Something for nothing, that's what they all wanted. And to think he had felt sorry for him. Well, he could call Greg a brownie or whatever they called it in a Negro slum. He would have the last laugh. Now where was Basil?

But Jake continued to make a point of the books with a surprising sincerity and politeness. "Do you . . . uh . . . always have that much homework?" he asked softly.

"I told you I had to bring home some extra ones. But . . . yeah . . . they keep us busy. Why? Don't you get any homework?"

"Heck, naw. What grade you in?"

"Eleventh."

"Like me." Jake shrugged his shoulders and swallowed. "Guess they think we ain't worth the bother."

"Who? What do you mean?"

29

"Aw, forget it."

Greg knew the boy regarded him as an outsider, but strangely enough he wanted to know what was troubling him. "Please tell me," he said softly, "what do you mean, you . . . we ain't . . . aren't worth the bother?"

"Kids at Cole don't do no homework. And even if they did, it'd be such a mess it wouldn't matter anyway."

"Aw, come on, Jake. Since when doesn't studying do any good?"

"Since black folks went to school."

To Jake that was it. He sipped his soda casually, satisfied that there was nothing more to say. Greg knew that if he didn't speak up quickly it would indeed be the end of something which perhaps could be the beginning. "Look, Jake, there's probably something to what you're saying, but you may be wrong about a few things, too. Tell me, what's it like when you go to school? What do you do all day?"

Jake studied Greg curiously and Greg saw that same expression he had seen once before in the Cole Rec locker room. It was as though Jake were making up his mind about something. "Well . . . down here we just don't take it serious. Down here . . . you go to school, your friends go to school, maybe your chick goes to school. You talk and mess around. Bell rings, you shuffle around a little bit, lunchtime comes, you go over to Duke's for a smoke. Sometimes the boss gives you homework—if he's not too busy messing around hisself—but, man, he's kidding. You dig it?"

"I think so."

"Then, you're sixteen and you move on out and make room for the next party."

"Anybody ever go to college?"

"Yeah. Once in a while. But that's a fluke. People say 'How about that?' like someone found a bag of money hid in the cellar, then they go on with they own business. I . . . I knowed a gal that went to business college once. She married a bum who left her with a kid. Then she went to New York City."

30

"Well, what about . . . you?"

"What about me?"

"You didn't quit school. And you must be sixteen."

"Almost seventeen."

"Well . . . what do you want to do?"

"It ain't what you want, man," Jake whined.

"Are you in shop like your brother was?"

"No."

"Regular high school?"

"Yeah."

"Typing, shorthand, and that. . . ."

"Academic."

Greg looked at Jake blankly, unsure that he was telling the truth.

"Yeah, yeah," Jake insisted.

"Well . . . why?"

Jake looked disgusted. He sighed. Greg knew the time was running out. "Why," Jake echoed deep down in his throat. "Typing and that stuff is for girls. Do I look like a girl?" Without waiting for an answer, "And I'm no good with my hands."

"Well . . . you must be pretty smart to be a junior and still be in academic. . . ."

"Yeah. Yeah," the colored boy piped.

"And you sound to me like you know what's happening and what you're supposed to do. . . ."

"Well, I'm glad you-all approve. 'Supposed to do.' Hmph. The trouble with you, boy, is you know all about 'supposed to do' but *nothing* about what's happening."

"What . . . what do you mean by that?"

"Don't act dumb with me! Now ain't it about time you're getting to work? What time you start anyway?"

Greg became angry. This guy wasn't doing him a favor, he thought. Then he felt a sudden rush of chagrin as he looked at the clock. Twenty to six. He was late. But darn if this . . . punk was going to shoo him on like an little old lady who found an errant school boy. He rose slowly and painstak-

31

ingly went through the motions of looking unconcerned with the time—checking his pockets for his wallet and pen, arranging his books in a neat pile, carefully folding his sport coat over his arm. When he was ready to leave, he said, "Yeah. I guess it is time for me to go. It was . . . interesting talking with you."

"Ssssheeee!"

"Maybe we can talk again sometime."

"Hmph."

"See you around." Greg walked to the door slowly. At least he hadn't been bested.

But when he was ready to walk out the door, Greg discovered that he really didn't care about that after all. Nobody had been around to see the show anyway. Instead, he had a vague feeling that something important had been left undone. And the next thing he knew, he was walking back. "Look," he said to the colored boy. "Why don't we meet after work? Have a coke or something?"

Jake looked surprised, then suspicious. "What for?"

"Just to talk. Come on. No sense going away mad."

Jake looked scornful now. "What you up to, asking me all these questions? You writing a paper on the Negro problem?"

Greg's face felt hot. "No." His throat was dry. "Nothing like that. Honest. I want to ask a couple of things, but in a friendly way. I don't mean anything by it."

Jake looked squarely into Greg's eyes. He was more trustful now, but at the same time, sad. "But why should I talk about that stuff?"

"Look. You could be wrong about a couple of things, you know. Now, come on. Give it a try. What've you got to lose?"

Jake waited and waited. "All right."

Greg could hardly believe he had agreed to it. "Well . . . good." He grabbed the boy by the arm and shook it. "Good. I'll see you at eight-thirty, then. That's when I'm done working. I've got to go now." He walked away briskly.

"Hey!"

Greg stopped and turned around.

"Where?"

"Uh . . . in front of the building."

Jake waved him on.

Greg ran toward the building as fast as he could. If he went around the back, it would look like he was trying to sneak in. Before he gave himself a chance to flounder outside of the building, he walked brazenly up the front steps. Whoever would see him would see him, that's all.

Mitzi was out on the landing at the bulletin board as he came up. "Well, hello," she said. "Did you get lost?"

"Sort of. Did you miss me?"

"I was counting the seconds!"

"How could I resist coming to this paradise with you here?"

She laughed. They had been kidding around like that for days now.

Greg went to the dressing stall and changed clothes. As he walked back out into the office, Doc's jumbo-sized, marked-up calendar stopped him. The circled "9" loomed out. It was the night of the dance. He was supposed to meet Virginia, not Jake, after work. Even if he could go back outside, he wouldn't know where to begin looking for Jake—too many minutes had passed to expect to find him close by.

There was a phone downstairs that he could use to call . . . Virginia; who else? Jake might not take it well after all the coaxing he had put up with. He would promise Virginia he'd take her dancing at The Meadowland tomorrow night instead. They'd get all dressed up; she'd like that.

It wasn't till an hour later that he got his chance; the kids in the game room were temporarily under control, Doc was nowhere in sight. He dropped a dime in the slot and dialed. Mrs. Ashburn answered the phone.

"Hello, Mrs. Ashburn. This is Greg. May I speak to Virginia?"

"Just a moment, dear."

"Hi, Greg."

33

"Hi, baby. . . ."

"Wait till you see the new sweater I'm wearing tonight. I had my eye on it all week and I just brought it home. It's a knockout. I'm so glad it got cool. . . ."

"Virginia. . . ."

"I could hardly keep from getting it for school this week. . . ."

"VIRGINIA. . . ."

"What?"

"I can't go tonight."

"What?" Virginia peeped at the other end of the line.

That helpless squeak of disbelief, thought Greg. Better if she had yelled. But . . . darn . . . this wasn't a prom, he told himself. "I said I can't go tonight. Something came up."

"Oh. Anything wrong at home?"

She would have to be thoughtful. "No, honey. Nothing like that. I just got some wires crossed. . . ."

"Are you sick?"

"No. I just . . . forgot and. . . ."

"Forgot??"

"Virginia, there's no sense in trying to explain it over the phone. Look. Tomorrow is my day off. I'll pick you up in the morning and we'll go for a drive and I'll explain things then."

"Well, what is it?"

"I said I can't explain now," said Greg. He was becoming jittery about being on the phone for so long. And Alphonse Green had come in and that always meant trouble. Now he was pulling Cassie Heard's braids and Cassie was starting to yell. "I've got to hang up."

"Everybody will be there. . . ."

"Stop worrying about 'everybody'! I . . . I'm sorry. Look. Why don't you go anyway. It's not a couples dance."

"I can take care of myself."

"All right. I've gotta go now. Kiss?"

A squeaky PFOP! came over the line. Greg returned it. Then he hung up with relief.

34

At eight-thirty Greg went to the staff room to change. Easier to just wear all these fancy threads instead of carrying them around, he thought. He stuffed his soiled work clothes into a paper bag.

"You look nice," Mitzi said when he came out. "Have a date?"

"With the boys," said Greg. "You look nice yourself." She had on a bright blue dress that repeated the color of her eyes, and in spite of her height, she stood proudly tall in high heels. Greg walked over and stood by her, checking her height against himself. Their eyes were on the same level and they laughed. "Where are you going?" asked Greg.

Mitzi sighed in mock despondency and limply held up her ringed hand. "I'm under lock and key, remember?"

They said good night to Doc and walked down the steps together. "Hi, Jake," Mitzi said.

"Hey. My gal Mitzi. How's the boss man? Ain't seen him around for a long time."

"He's fine, Jake. Just busy at school. Anybody need a lift?"

"Naw. We just messing around."

"You two going out together?"

"Y-e-e-eah."

"Well, good night. Behave yourselves." She walked away and opened a car door.

"You know her?" asked Greg.

"Aw yeah. Knowed her before you. She's real foxy. You know Big Roy?"

"Her fiancé?"

"Yeah."

"No, I never met him. Does he come around here?"

"Yeah."

Then they were silent. It was a mild, clear night. And quiet. No traffic on the avenue now. It was awkwardly quiet. Both Greg and Jake were struck with the same realization

35

that they were strangers to each other and that Greg was a
stranger to Cole. "Everything looks closed around here," said
Greg.

"Yeah. I know a place . . . up the hill," said Jake uncertainly.

"It's okay with me."

Jake took some of Greg's books and they started up the
hill. In a little while Jake nodded at a frail, yellow-shingled
house propped on the sloping street. "My pad," he said, and
they continued up the buckling sidewalk.

Soon they were at an important looking street amply
spotted with narrow eating places, bars, laundromats, gro-
cery stores and amusement arcades. People sat out in front
of practically every building and hung out from windows as
well. Greg realized that this was Rydberg Avenue and
became tense. There was news about Rydberg Avenue in the
paper every now and then, news about things like fights,
raids and robberies. Right now, Greg thought, the place
looked too bright and populous for anything to happen, but
you could never tell. He felt more relieved as a patrol car
cruised by and especially when he saw that no one took
much notice of him.

He began to feel a little giddy, in fact. Loud, rhythmic
blues from one speaker blended with that of another, and
the whole street pulsed with a continuum of music, loud talk
and laughter. The sidewalks were crowded with sharpies in
suits, ties and hats, young sharp chicks in snug, bright
clothes, and housewives in loose dresses and floppy shoes.

In a little while they came to a place called Sophie's Grill
which appeared to accommodate a young crowd. "This is
it," said Jake. Greg had mixed feelings on seeing a few familiar faces from the park; he wasn't sure he wanted to be
recognized. The fat girl was there, the one with the thick
wide-spaced teeth who always wore orange. She was bend-
ing and bowing and lolling to the music like a great pumpkin
in a Hallowe'en parade.

"Who is that girl?" said Greg.

36

"You mean Big Patty. Patty Dawkins. I play ball with her brother Dumbo," said Jake.

Sophie's Grill was a large hall cheaply furnished with things from junk stores—old chrome and plastic kitchen furniture in various colors and styles. Cheap yellow linoleum with green rectangles pointing this way and that covered the floor; it was dog-eared around the edges and battered through to the back. Near the entrance was a counter with torn red plastic stools where Sophie herself gave the service. She was a homely, husky white woman with a perpetual scowl. Her large black eyes darted about the room suspiciously as she scrubbed and wiped and filled glasses, and when she reached over the counter top, she displayed thick strong arms. The hall was poorly illuminated by low-watt bulbs peeking from green poolroom shades, and it took a while to get accustomed to the semi-darkness. But you forgot about the shabbiness after a while, Greg thought, because everyone seemed to be having a good time.

Greg heard small jazz and rock'n roll combos, the kind he listened to occasionally on the local Negro radio station, while two pinball machines beat out an incongruous rhythm of their own.

They sat silently, Greg and Jake, listening to the flashing juke box rumble a slow, sensuous wail of female voices—

> *Is it i-in his eyes?*
> *O-oh, no, no, no;*
> *Is it i-in his arms?*
> *O-oh, no, no, no. . . .*

And the whole room throbbed with rhythm. The dancers bent and swayed in one churning wave. The undulating brown bodies lent an added physical dimension to the tunes and Greg felt excited.

But Jake reminded him why they were there and broke the spell. "Well . . . what did you want to talk about?" he asked.

It hardly seemed the right place to talk about serious things, but after all the coaxing, Greg didn't want Jake to feel he was wasting his time. "I was enjoying myself," he began.

"Good," said Jake. And he didn't seem impatient or unfriendly.

"Well . . . what we were talking about before. . . ."

"Yeah?"

"Oh . . . I was just wondering what you like in school. I don't mean what you think of the teachers or anything like that, but what subjects you like."

"Mm. I like science, I guess. I liked geometry." Jake's eyes bulged and he ran his hand nervously over his head. "Last year I took biology—liked that. This year I have chemistry. Like that. Sometimes it's a drag. In lab they take all day to do one simple thing. I could do it faster if nobody was around bossin'. I don't know. What do you like?"

"History. I'd like to major in it in college."

"You all set to go to college, huh?"

"Yes."

"Hm."

"And you? With the academic course. . . ."

"That ain't the reason. I told you. What else was I gonna do?" He was still rubbing his hand back and forth over his head; it was automatic, almost like a machine, but there was a tenseness in his brown arm. "Thought maybe I could get a job as a lab helper or something. What's there to talk about? You do what you like best while you're in the place."

"Didn't you ever even think about going to college?"

Jake frowned at Greg and turned away wordlessly.

"There . . . there are a lot of . . . of Negroes who go, you know."

For a while it seemed like Jake didn't even care to talk, but he finally replied. "It takes bread, man. And it takes some other things, too."

"Well . . . what about those Negroes right up the avenue? The ones who're doctors and lawyers?"

"They have money, man. Look, there was a time when a man—even a colored boy—could get a job."

38

"Well . . . I guess you're right about that. But you could work your way through by getting a job at the school. And you'd be amazed at the scholarships you can get."

"Well, they ain't gonna give a colored boy no scholarship. Whitey doesn't want the black boy to go to school anyway; don't you know that?"

Greg reddened and he was glad that he had a good quick answer. "For your information, there are special scholarships just for Negroes. Doesn't your school counselor tell you about these things?"

"The counselor? You mean old Sourballs Meers? Is that what that cat's for? Shoot! I thought he was for expelling people. He's so mean people are scareder of him than the principal. When you get in trouble you get sent to him. I didn't know that's what he was for. If I'da known that's what he was for, I'da . . . complained."

"Well, he must have notices and stuff posted on his bulletin board."

"I never saw none. Besides, I couldn't get a scholarship."

"Why not?"

"My marks."

"Didn't you say. . . . I thought. . . . Something you said this afternoon made me think you . . . you did all right."

"Well, I do most of the time. But it's English. I hate it."

"What's the trouble?"

"Well, I think I say good things in composition. Smart things. But the teacher, she always writes 'fundamentals poor' and that's that. Shoot, I don't even think she reads what I say. Grammar is all she cares about, and . . . well . . . you know how I talk."

Greg checked a ready inclination to agree and said, "It's not too late to work on it, though."

"Aw, I don't know. What for? It's all part of the scene. It's my bag."

"Well . . . maybe you ought to be thinking about changing the scene. Or quitting the bag."

39

"Wasn't my idea to get in it," said Jake. "I got drafted."
And he threw his head back and out came that voiceless,
wheezy laugh. "And maybe you better cool it, baby." And
laughed some more.

———

It was ten o'clock and time for another moonlight dance.
Meadowland Palace grew darker and the multi-faceted, mir-
rored globe revolving in the center of the ceiling caught the
light and whirled cheap stars around the room. Greg held
Virginia close and smiled at the scent of roses from her hair.
As they glided along the glass wall, Greg felt warm ripples
of pleasure. At times like this, it was a joy to just . . . exist, to
be silent, mindless, all physical; to passively, effortlessly ab-
sorb all the sensory pleasures of nature and man—sweet
smells, music, cozy shelter from a cool outdoors, a pretty
girl.

But dance number six was soon over. The lights came on
and with them came the shuffling and mumbling of people
very much aware of themselves and oblivious to the opiates
of a danceland. Dancers politely but awkwardly abandoned
old partners, the girls excused themselves to the powder
room; the boys leaning forward with mumbled thank-you's.
Young people along the walls roved again, looking for imaginary friends. Virginia moved close to Greg and took his
hand.

"Gre-eg," she chided. "You didn't even say anything about
my new dress."

"Oh. I'm sorry. I noticed it all right. But you know how it
is. Sometimes you see something and you think about it but
you never make the words come out." He stepped back and
looked and mumbled. "Uh-huh. Nice. Sure is a crazy little
thing. Let's go out and take a closer look. I'm thirsty."

They walked into the snack bar. Greg studied the dress
while Virginia struck poses. It was a black knitted tube that

wrapped her from her knees up to under her arms, with thick straps crossing her back. "It is . . . odd, Virginia," said Greg. "I'm not saying I don't like it—on you it looks good—but it is . . . odd. Sort of like a sock." Virginia giggled. "Like one of those sock dolls. That's what you look like."

"A sock doll? Oh!" Virginia scolded playfully.

"But you're the sexiest sock doll I ever saw."

"All right, Greg Davis. You saved yourself this time. Now where were you last night?"

"Why didn't you go for a drive with me this morning? I told you I'd tell you then."

"I had to have my hair done for tonight. Like it?"

"Looks nice."

"Well, where were you? You're stalling."

"I was with a friend . . . a fellow I met at the park. Jake—that fellow I told you about. The one that called off the wolves."

"You mean that colored boy?"

"Yeah."

"What on earth for?"

"Well . . . I ran into him at a restaurant right before work and we started to talk. One thing led to another, and pretty soon we were having a serious discussion."

"What on earth would you have to discuss with him?"

"School. Himself. Some other things. He's different from us, the way he talks, the way he thinks. . . ."

"No kidding!"

"Now wait. It's not as simple as you think. He seems like a pretty decent guy and he's not dumb. But he's missing out on things just because he doesn't know what's going on."

"I don't know what you're talking about."

"Well, he doesn't think he's a big deal like we think we are. We're going to do this, we're going to do that. . . ."

"That's just what they say about Negroes. That they live for today and have no ambition."

"Who says?"

41

"I know there are exceptions, but this guy sounds just like . . . a typical Negro. Most of them are . . . well . . . worthless, and this guy is already washed up, too."

"Well, they're not born that way. There are reasons."

"Of course there are reasons. Biological make up, just as in every living thing. Some strains are born stronger and more intelligent. . . ."

"Where did you dig up that pseudo stuff?"

"From Mona's father. One day when I was there he was talking about it with one of his business associates. They were saying how shiftless and lazy and incapable the Negro workers were. . . ."

"Garbage. What does he know?"

"He hires them, remember? And I think he's a very intelligent man. He reads a lot."

"He's a big mouth like Rich, that's for sure. I met him and I don't like him. He's as cold as a dead fish. He was pretty nasty to Rich's mother when I was there. And as for being smart, I don't know. My father says something completely different, and he oughta know. He studied that stuff. Perhaps if every day of your life was as miserable as theirs, you wouldn't want to think about the next one, either."

"Well, your father's a social worker, and I guess if he didn't think like that he wouldn't be one in the first place."

"Well, Rich's father has a store on Cole Avenue, and if he didn't try to tell everybody, including himself, that Negroes were no good, he couldn't pay them low wages. . . ."

"Ooooo, listen to him! You'd better shut up. You're getting awfully personal. You can't go around saying things about people like that."

"Well . . . you started it. Guess I have a temper. Let's forget the whole thing, huh?"

"I agree. But if you don't mind my noticing, you seem awfully involved with this . . . Jake."

"No. I hardly know him. It's just that . . . I guess I feel a little sorry for him. Yeah. Maybe I ought to try to get to know him a little better."

42

"Oh, come on. They're not paying you to rehabilitate them down there."

"Well, maybe I want to. I can pick my own friends. I don't like to have them dumped on me."

"What do you mean by that?"

"I . . . I don't know. Let's forget it."

"All right. Let's not fight. Where did you go with Jake?"

"We went to a place where some of his gang loaf. Up on Rydberg Avenue. . . ."

Virginia stared. "Are you crazy?"

Greg smiled. She sounded just like his mother had last night. "I guess it was a little foolish. But last night I never even thought of it. Everything around the park was closed, so I left it up to him to suggest a place."

"Weren't you even afraid?"

"A little, at times. But it turned out all right."

"Hmm. I'll bet that place was pretty wild, huh?"

"Sophie's?"

"Wherever you went."

"It was kind of beat up. But it was a lot of fun."

"I'll bet. I would have liked to have seen *that*."

"What?"

"The way they danced and all."

Greg shrugged his shoulders. "Just look around you."

"Oh, come on, Greg. Don't act dumb. They're more sensuous and uninhibited than white people, aren't they?"

"Oh. That. Yeah. And when they did the Watusi they painted their faces and put bones through their noses."

"You don't have to get so smart."

"Well cool it, baby. You're always looking for something sensational."

"Oh, stop acting so superior. And you don't have to embarrass me. Let's go back in and dance."

"That's what I say."

43

FRIENDSHIP

Tuesday again, and Greg rushed into Cole Rec and changed his clothes. "Greg," said Mitzi as he was leaving the office, "will you please put these posters on the bulletin board?"

"Anything for you," said Greg. Mitzi smiled. He took the four posters—green, blue, pink and yellow—and walked out onto the landing. The first one was about a swimming meet at Hampton Rec where his cousin Kathy swam. He took down the out-of-date orange one about the summer meet and tacked the new one up. The pink one which said something about a beauty and charm class that would meet on Saturday mornings could go below it. He searched for a spot for the blue sign. He pressed the tack into the corner near the gym schedule—there. Then he stepped back.

"Ow!" Right on someone's foot.

"Sorry!" Greg wheeled around swiftly. "Oh, it's you, Jake. Oh. And your shoes are off. Foot all right?"

"I'll live," said Jake. "Whatcha got here?" They both looked at the blue poster.

MANSFIELD WINTER SCIENCE FAIR
DECEMBER 14-31
$2000 IN PRIZES
COLLECTIONS DISPLAYS MODELS
DETAILS AND REGISTRATION AT YOUR HIGH SCHOOL

Jake scratched his head. "Two thousand bucks. Mmm-HMM! That's some ni-i-ice bread." He studied the sign so intently Greg couldn't help feeling surprised; the yellow sign was still tucked under his arm. "Wonder how many prizes that two thousand bones has to cover."

"I couldn't tell you, Jake. Are you interested in this thing?"

"Well, I have a collection," said Jake.

"You??"

The colored boy frowned. "Why not?"

"Oh . . . I don't know. It's just funny, a big guy like you."

"Well, it's true."

"What kind of a collection?"

"Insects. Mostly beetles."

Greg still wasn't sure that Jake wasn't putting him on again. "What would you be doing with a bug collection?"

"It's like this, baby: when we lived back on Langley Avenue, I didn't have any friends except the ones that came in and out of the walls. I was so lonely, I zapped them up."

"Aw!"

"I'm not jiving you," Jake shouted jubilantly. "We had all kinds of things there. My aunt used to call them all roaches, so I quit asking her what they was and went out and got a fifteen-cent picture book of them. One thing led to another and pretty soon I was mounting them. Aunt Sallie really got shook up then. She used to make me stay in the cellar, then she took me to some palm readers and astrologers, then to church. Then she said I was demonized and got used to it and gave up. That was a couple of years ago. Haven't done much on it since then. But I still have the stuff. Done a good job on them. Now. Don't you think I could make up something for this here"—Jake looked back at the poster—"science fair thing? Make some drawings and enter it?"

"I don't know. I guess." It had all begun to sound on the level.

45

"My old biology teacher wasn't such a bad babe, come to think of it. I think she liked me. Maybe she'd help."

"I should think so. She could probably tell you if your . . . collection's any good."

"Eh . . . I might as well forget it. I'd probably need all kinds of special stuff."

"Now wait. Couldn't you get supplies at school? And build things like showcases in the shop?"

"Can't stay in school all day, man. They close up at three-thirty."

"Don't they give you an hour or so to work after school? Keep the shops open?" Burnside had an active student body, and services and facilities were available to them after classes.

"Not at Cole," said Jake.

"What about your free periods? Study halls?"

"Don't have that much time. Besides, nobody wants to be bothered."

"Well . . . what do you think you'd need?"

"Showcases, like you said. Glass, I guess. My stuff's just mounted in boxes now. Stains. I don't know until I look into it. A microscope maybe. Maybe not."

"You could use mine," Greg said automatically, remembering the thing stored in the cellar. Only after the words had tumbled out of his mouth did Greg realize he had made the invitation.

"Your what?" said Jake.

"Microscope."

"You have your own microscope?"

"Yes. It's a pretty good one, I think. I never used it much."

"Did your folks buy it for you?"

"One of my aunts. She's married to a biologist and she never had any kids. I'm her favorite nephew. She bought it for me when I was twelve."

"You sure are lucky." Jake looked wistfully at the floor. He seemed so caught up with the idea that Greg wondered whether or not he had heard his invitation.

46

"You say you don't even use it?"

Greg reddened. Everybody couldn't flip over bugs, he thought. "No, I don't. Guess I never will."

"Ever think of selling it?"

"Yeah. I guess."

"How much did it cost?"

"Oh . . . around seventy bucks, I guess."

"Oo-ee!"

"They probably have better models by now. I'd sell it much cheaper."

"Don't look at me. I don't have any money," said Jake. And underneath the blustering there was a touch of chagrin.

Greg knew what he must say but he shrank from speaking. He had so many qualms now—his parents' feelings, letting the expensive tool go. But these qualms he understood. It was the strange fears he did not recognize that bothered him—vague ones about his security and privacy, about becoming involved in . . . he didn't even know what. He knew he had been standing silent a long time but he repeated what he knew was the right thing to say. "There's no reason why you can't borrow it, Jake, if you want to look into this science fair."

"How do you mean?"

Greg was still uncomfortable; stupid question—"How do you mean?" "Take a look at it; see if it's any good; and if you think you can use it, take it home."

"Take it . . . ? Aw, I don't know. If I can't give you something, I'd rather not."

"Don't be like that. Look, there's no sense in cutting your own neck and not entering because you won't use a microscope that's just rotting in someone's cellar. Even if you don't win a thing, it won't hurt you to try instead of just giving up."

"I know. I know," Jake said softly. He stood quietly for a long time, running his hand nervously over his head. Greg glanced at the clock. It was a quarter to six. Doc would be

47

wondering why it took so long to stick up a few signs. Jake always had to complicate things.

"Look," said Greg. "Why don't you come over this weekend and look at it? Bring some of your own stuff if you want. What do you say?" Jake looked surprised. "All right?"

"Can't you bring it down here? I . . . I'm sorry. I guess that sounds pretty ignorant. What I mean is, maybe you'd rather bring it here than . . . than. . . ." Jake looked at Greg nervously, hoping Greg would spare him the ordeal of speaking his fears. But Greg had nothing to say and Jake was forced to finish. "Than me come up to your pad—know what I mean?"

Greg still didn't know what to say. He tried to pretend that he couldn't understand Jake's reservations. "But maybe you won't even want it, and I'd just have to carry it around. It's pretty delicate, you know."

"Okay. If you're sure it's all right. I mean, maybe . . . maybe your folks'll get mad, me coming up to your pad. Look, maybe you want to forget the whole thing. I'm busy anyway. . . ."

"I said for you to come, didn't I?" Greg snapped. Ten to six. It was hard enough without Jake making things worse. "Look, I can't make arrangements with you now. I'm late getting to work. Will you be around Friday?"

"I don't know."

"Well, stop around, huh?" Greg demanded.

"All right. I gotta go now. Want to get in some shots before the boys come." Jake turned and disappeared into the gym.

A rush of helplessness welled up in Greg. HE'S gotta go? he thought angrily as he punched a tack through the last poster. He jogged into the gym. Doc had his back turned. He speeded through the exit.

Jake, dragging himself down the stairs with curious slowness today, still hadn't reached the locker room. He turned on hearing the noise behind him. On his face was a strange, sad look.

48

"I have to open the door, you know," said Greg.

———✐———

It was a still, lazy Sunday afternoon, and the street was deserted. Greg found himself taking special notice of the emptiness. Perhaps, he thought, he had been a little too sensitive about the whole thing, about bringing a colored person to his home. He looked again at the bare street, the empty windows. The bus would be along any minute and it looked as if no one cared after all.

It had been just like that the other night, when he worriedly asked his father how he thought his mother would feel about having Jake at the house on Sunday afternoon. When Mr. Davis assured him that she wouldn't care in the least, he had felt a little ashamed for expecting the worst of her. He should have known. Mom and Dad were anything but prejudiced.

Then he thought of the previous evening and smiled at a coincidence. It had been the night of the Civic League's fall variety show, and Mag Bryce had approached the family during the intermission, selling tickets to the Orphans Benefit Christmas Ball. She had rushed over like a giddy chicken, genuinely friendly and really meaning well, clucking, "Gregory! Is this your family? How lovely!" He had introduced everybody and Mag cooed and rumpled his little sister's hair. "Wasn't Virginia simply lovely?" she squealed, and everyone hummed in agreement. Then she proceeded to peddle the tickets.

They chatted for a few minutes about the orphanage and about the fact that a good many of its children were colored. "How heartwarming it is to see their happy little faces," Mag had said, "brown faces, black faces, and white faces, too, all bright with excitement. Tragic enough that some of them have had the nurturing in a home destroyed through natural causes. But some of them—particularly the Negro children," she had whispered, "have never even known legitimate parents. It seems to be a hopeless pattern, and the best we can do is light this one little candle. I always say it's the parents who should be called illegitimate, not the children. Wouldn't you say so, Mr. Davis, being in social work?"

The assistant supervisor of the orphanage, Mr. Armstrong, was a Negro, and Mag clucked on about how she invited him to her home for dinner "along with the other people" some time after the ball, when the proceeds were handed over to him. "I don't hedge about these things," she had said. "We have cocktails together, eat together, and have a perfectly lovely time. Mr. Armstrong is a fine Negro man, a true gentleman. There's no reason why they shouldn't all turn out as well."

Well, then, Greg thought. If Mag could invite a Negro over, then so could he. Maybe she'd even be pleased if she happened to be gazing out from behind the curtains in one of the empty-looking windows all around him. What would she really think?

The bus passed by and Greg was stunned. No Jake. He felt at once confused and worried. But in a few moments he spotted the familiar, tall dark figure crossing the street. "Did you get off at the wrong stop?" he hollered as he went over to meet the boy.

"Nope. I walked here."

"All the way from your house?" It was at least an hour walk.

"Yeah. I'm the world's boss walker, man. I felt like walking through where the fancy blacks live, and by the time I did that, I was halfway here."

"Hmm. It's such a long walk, though, and it's so hot today."

"Yeah, that's the thing. I made myself thirsty. Is there any place . . . ? Well . . . we'd better get on with it."

"Did you want to stop off for something to drink?"

"Naw, naw. I'll live."

"There's a place pretty close."

"Forget it."

50

"Well, I think it's a good idea. I walked here myself. I had to get something at the store for my mother."

"Sure you don't mind? You don't have to. . . ."

"No. Come on. Let's go." Greg tried not to acknowledge Jake's shyness. John McGinnis' drugstore was about three blocks away. "This is one of our hangouts," Greg explained as they approached the huge drug and confectionery store. "Some of the kids from my high school loaf around here."

As they entered, the crisp, cool air-conditioning instantly refreshed their bodies. They rounded the cashier and tobacco stall, entered the blue annex, and sat down in a booth. There was a minimum booth charge of twenty-five cents per person, so Greg went up to Skippy Sullivan, who was at the counter, and ordered two lemon sodas. He sat down to wait for them on a stool.

"Who's your friend?" asked Skip as he bent over the vanilla ice cream tank and dug with the scoop.

"His name's Jake. Met him at work."

"Where you workin' now, Davis?"

"The recreation center on Cole Avenue."

"Oh, yeah. Somebody said. They give you homework?" Skip cackled in a malicious pitch.

"No," said Greg.

"Maybe he wants chocolate?" Skip mumbled and laughed.

"Cut the funny stuff and just finish the sodas."

In a short time the two boys were eagerly downing the sodas and talking about sports; both were reluctant to continue on the way. Jake asked Greg if he had seen the Eagles' game on television the previous afternoon. When Greg said no, he had had to work, the conversation stopped. He looked out over Jake's head, not knowing where to look, and just then he saw Rich Wallace and Frank Klinglehaus. What were they doing here at this time on Sunday afternoon? Greg wondered. They were dressed in suits. Frank spotted his friend and came over to the booth.

"Hi," said Greg. "What're you guys all dressed up for?"

"We just came from church," said Frank.

Greg looked at his watch in an obvious way. "Lazy man's services?" he said. It was one-thirty.

"Men's Youth Organization meeting," Frank explained. "We had to stick around."

"Well sit down." Greg slid over in his seat and Jake did the same.

Rich pulled away from the booth. "We'll go over by the window," he said. "We have some things to talk over." He walked away and Frank followed, mumbling, "See you tomorrow, Greg."

"Yeah. See you at practice, Davis," said Rich.

"They're on Burnside's basketball team, too," Greg said when they were gone.

" 'Too'? You . . . ?"

"I guess I never mentioned it. . . ."

"What's your last name again?"

"Davis."

Jake snapped his fingers. "Davis. Yeah. Yeah. Greg Davis. Hey. Put it here." They shook hands over the table.

"I'm famous?"

"Heard your name on the radio a couple times last year during the playoffs. You were a scrub."

"You must really follow sports."

"I like 'em."

"We'd better shove off. My mother has dinner early on Sundays."

—————✦—————

First meetings were always so stiff, Greg thought as they sat at the dinner table. It had been this way every other time he had brought a new friend to the house, yet today it was different. Greg felt edgy. He wished Betsy, his seven-year-old sister, would stop staring at Jake even though it was simply a child's reaction to a new person and Betsy did it to everyone. But Greg couldn't help making much of the fact that Jake glanced nervously at her now and then as she held her steady, serious gaze.

He sighed. What an ordeal. It must have been even worse for Jake. The family always asked his friends the same old stupid questions: what do you like in school? Ya-ta-ta; ya-ta-ta. And Jake uttered short replies, mostly "Yes, ma'm" and "No, ma'm," and tried desperately to keep up his part in the conversation. So ordinary a routine, meeting someone's parents; yet Jake lacked that amused, assured respect for formalities that everyone else seemed to have. Instead, he seemed defensive and genuinely afraid.

When the small talk finally fizzled out, Greg said, "What do you say, Jake? Want to go down to the basement and look at the big eye?" Jake nodded and seemed relieved.

"Mmm. Nice cellar you have," he said when they were downstairs. "You should see ours. Like a coal mine. Black and all dirt and you think the steps are gonna fall down and you'll get buried alive."

"It's this one," Greg said as he took down a box. Jake helped him lower it. Greg untied the rope and lifted the flap, revealing a yellow tangle of excelsior and more cardboard packing.

"Looks like you never opened it," said Jake.

"That's pretty much the truth."

Greg pushed the packing aside, and as Jake stared, lifted out an irregularly-shaped black leather case about sixteen inches long. He opened some snaps and uncovered the microscope.

Jake gaped. "That thing ain't been touched."

"Well . . . as I said . . . I got it in the seventh grade, and I wasn't taking science or anything. Didn't know how to use it."

"Mm-HMM! What I wouldn't do with a thing like this. Where are the slides?"

"There's some more stuff down here," Greg mumbled as he dug into the box. "Here's a book. And a box of slides. Some parts. . . ."

Jake was already looking for a place where he could set up the instrument; in a short time he was reading the booklet. "Magnifies!" He whistled. "This thing is pretty powerful. Betcha' I could magnify parts of insects and make blown-up sketches."

"With a camera?"

"No. I don't have one. But I could draw 'em."

"You could borrow mine." Greg said.

"Never mind. Never mind. You don't learn how to be a scientific photographer by just gettin' a camera no matter how good it is."

"Do you draw very well?"

"Good enough. I was always pretty good at drawing."

For the next half hour, Greg looked on while Jake was busy with the microscope. He acted like Greg wasn't even there, except to call him over once in a while to look at something. At times Greg caught Jake's enthusiasm; at other times he was restless. "Well? What do you think?" he asked the colored boy after a while.

"I'd sure like to work with it, but I have no collateral."

"I already told you you could borrow it."

"What your folks gonna say about that? This ain't a cheap piece of junk."

"I know you'd take care of it."

"I know I would, too. There's no kids at my house. Aunt Sallie never touches my stuff whether she agrees with it or not. You could come and see for yourself."

"I'd like to do that. I mean . . . not check on it, but I'd like to see how you progress with the project."

"You would?"

"Sure. Maybe I can drop by next weekend after work."

"That soon? I . . . I'm sorry."

"Well, you'd better get started on it."

"I will. I will."

Greg drove Jake home with the big box. They came to the wobbly yellow-shingled house. "Well here's my digs by day-

54

light," said Jake. "Do you . . . uh . . . want to come in for a cup of coffee?"

Greg didn't want to offend him, but he did have things to do. He looked at his watch. "It's almost six, Jake, and I have some homework to do. Gotta call the chick, too. We'll make it Friday, okay? I'll talk to you at the park on Tuesday." Jake looked relieved.

When Greg pulled away, he noticed Jake through the rear-view mirror. The boy stood on the curb, the big box in his hands, just looking after him.

It was drizzling as Greg walked to the athletics building after school on Monday, and the strain of holding up an umbrella with two armfuls of books reminded him of the burdens of the coming cold season. Soon there would be boots and scarves. "Hey, Greg. Wait up," came a voice from behind. It was Frank Klinglehaus trotting over in the rain. Now it was pouring. "Let's have some of that umbrella," said Frank.

"Take it. You carry it."

"Too bad about that English assignment, huh?" said Frank.

Greg shrugged his shoulders.

"With the game and all this weekend?"

"It's only an exhibition game."

"Still—practice today, Wednesday, Friday, the game on Saturday—that doesn't leave much time. And Watson doesn't fool around with late themes. Last year Rich took an extra weekend to finish one that was due on a Friday; he lost a letter grade."

"I guess she doesn't have school spirit."

"Say, Greg?" said Frank as he closed the umbrella.

"What?"

"Who was that colored guy you were with in McGinnis' yesterday?"

55

Greg recalled how abruptly Frank and Rich had left the booth. "If you would have stuck around, I'd have introduced you."

"Well you know how Rich is. Who was he?"

"A fellow I met at work." They pushed open the doors to the locker room.

"What was he doing up here?"

"He came to see me. He came to look at a microscope I have."

"What for?"

"He wants to use it for something. For that science fair— you know, the one Marilyn got the chemistry award in last year."

"Couldn't you take it down to Cole?"

"Wha . . . ? Well, what for? Who wants to carry a thing like that all over town? Why shouldn't he come up here?"

"I didn't mean anything, Greg. But I couldn't help noticing. You never see them up here."

"Well, maybe it's about time you did."

"Don't get sore. Heck, I don't care. You think I'm like Rich?"

"Rich? What'd Loudmouth say?"

"He said. . . ." Frankie started to chuckle uncontrollably. "Oh, it was funny. . . ."

"Well, maybe you'd better not tell me."

"It was funny."

"Forget it."

"You always laughed before."

"That was different. That wasn't about anybody."

"Aw, I'm sorry, Greg. And . . . take it easy, huh. Rich doesn't even know your . . . friend, so how could what he says mean anything?"

"It's all right, Frank." Actually Frank was a pretty nice guy, thought Greg. One of his best friends, in fact. They double dated a lot.

"Now come on. We've been gassing here and we're late."

When they entered the gym, Rich and the rest of the team

were huddled with coach McKing. "Davis! Klingle!" Rich shouted. "Let's go! You're holding us back."

The moon illuminated the slummy neighborhood well as Jake and Greg made their way up the hill on Friday night. Such a congested neighborhood, thought Greg. Peeling, red-painted houses with sagging wooden steps leading up to the front doors were separated occasionally by black alleys. At Jake's yellow-shingled house they stopped by such an alley, and he said, "We have to go around the back. We live on the second floor."

They moved through perfect blackness; the moon was behind them now so there was no light to show the way through the alley. Greg extended his fingertips to touch the walls. "Still with me?" Jake asked good-naturedly. Greg was glad he was in a good mood.

Finally they came out into a small backyard. The brick walk was buckled and Greg almost tripped. Against a fence were two brimming rubbish barrels. The yard was smothered all around by more three-story buildings. Jake led Greg up steep rotting steps that rocked as their feet pounded on them. "Don't worry," said Jake. "They won't collapse."

They reached a small landing and Jake peered into a lighted window. "Aunt Sallie's readin' the paper," he said. "I told her you were coming. I told her who you were." Greg wondered what he meant. Jake rattled the knob of the heavy door. It opened as much as a safety chain allowed. "Me, Aunt Sal." Then the door swung open wide and a portly Negro woman with a square, stern face appeared and stepped back. "This is Greg Davis, Aunt Sal. My aunt, Greg. She says she knows your dad."

"How do you do?" said Greg, extending his hand.

The woman did not offer hers. She grunted "Hi" and stared coldly into Greg's eyes. Jake said, "Wait and I'll see if my dad's sleeping," and he disappeared behind a flowered curtain into the next room. Greg dreaded being left alone with the woman. She had her back turned to him and was busy at the refrigerator taking out a bag. All too soon she closed the refrigerator door and turned facing him, so that he felt the demands of cordiality in her hostile presence. To his relief she shouted "Bring me my coat, Jake," giving him an opportunity to break the ice.

"Going out?" he said.

"To work," she answered gruffly. And a tense silence hung over the room again.

"Come on in here, Greg," Jake called from the other room. Greg was glad to leave Aunt Sallie and he entered the small, dark parlor illuminated by a portable television set. Stretched out on the couch was a stout Negro man watching a detective program. "Sometimes Dad falls asleep on the couch," said Jake.

"Mine too."

The man said hello cheerfully and continued staring at the screen. It was obvious that he did not intend to carry on a conversation, but he didn't strike Greg as being unfriendly. Greg sat in a hard-backed chair at the foot of the couch and gazed absently at the program. But suddenly his senses were alerted by whispers.

"What's he want heah?" Aunt Sallie was rasping.

"Aw, Aunt Sal. Don't be like that."

"We ain't on welfare no more. He have nothin' to spy on here. We earnin' our own bread."

"He didn't come here to spy. What's there to see anyway?"

"That's what I'm askin' you, boy. It sure ain't cause he likes you."

"We talked about that already. I told you, he did come to see me. To look at my collection."

"To see you?" Aunt Sallie squealed. "Oo-ee! That boy out there would jus's soon break your black back as look at you."

"Don't talk like that!" Jake said angrily. By now their voices were audible.

"Well, I gotta go to work now. Somebody gotta work in this family," Aunt Sally muttered. "Ain't got time to hang around here playin' with bugs like some fools I know." Greg heard the door open. "No wonder the white folks think the black is a bunch of fools. I think so, too!" The door slammed shut.

"Greg?" Jake hollered from the kitchen.

"Yeah?"

"In here."

Greg swiped the curtain aside and entered the kitchen, pretending he hadn't heard anything. But Jake knew he had and was ready to air things out. "Don't mind Aunt Sal," he said.

"I don't think she likes me," said Greg nervously.

"Well . . . don't take it personal, fella. Aunt Sallie's had her troubles, too. So she has this thing about white people."

"ALL white people?"

"Sort of like the shoe being on the other foot, huh?"

"Yes. I . . . I never thought of it," said Greg. Jake turned away in disgust. "Do many colored people feel that way?"

"More'n some white folks think, it looks like."

"But take Mansfield. Mansfield's not like some places we know of, where there are klans, and discrimination in voting, and job problems. Sorry. Is it because of Danny that your aunt feels like that?"

"Hmph. That's only one reason. She has lots of reasons. Reasons going way back to when she was a kid and lived in the South. And then there was the thing that happened to Aunt Lizbeth. See, Aunt Sal and Dad had a kid sister. . . ."

"If it's something personal, forget it."

"It's no big secret. Well, Aunt Lizbeth was a sharp gal. Smart, too. She went to business college and was a secretary and dressed real fine and all. So one of the guys in the office —a white guy—had eyes for her. They started to go out together and pretty soon he wanted to marry her. Aunt Sallie didn't like it at all. She said he was just. . . . Well, I won't say it. But Aunt Lizbeth had a mind of her own. So one day

59

we got a telephone call—this was at our place on Langley Avenue. I remember it. I was four years old. It was right after my mother died. They were far away and they said they were getting married and they would give Dad and Aunt Sallie their last chance to be witnesses. Aunt Sallie said she was going to make sure nothing funny was being pulled off, so she dragged me and Danny and Dad, and off we went to the wedding."

"So Aunt Sallie has a grudge because she married a white man?"

"Well that ain't all of it."

"No?"

"No. They kept pretty much to themselves after that. Aunt Sal hardly knew their whereabouts. And she wasn't about to chase them. A couple of years later the guy was up for a good job and went to Chicago for an interview and just never came back. Aunt Lizbeth was going to have a baby, too."

"Did he know about that?"

"We don't know. Aunt Lizbeth was a proud girl and stubborn and she wouldn't tell us a thing."

"Then what happened to her?"

"She's in New York. She's been there for about ten years now."

"Ever hear from her?"

"Once in a while she sends a letter. Sometimes she sends me some scratch for my birthday. She has a pretty good job, I guess. Sonny's in school."

"Why did she go there?"

"Because she thought her friends would laugh, naturally. Besides, she always liked the big town anyway. She always was a swinger and had lots of fellas." Jake became angry. "She didn't have to marry that cracker. I really liked her. She took me and Danny to the movies. Bought us stuff. And that lousy...."

"Did you ever try to trace him?"

"We didn't know anything about it till it was too late. Do

60

you think those white folks where he worked were gonna say anything? Do you?" Jake demanded.

"I . . . I don't know. I guess not. It sure is a sad. . . ."

"Yeah. It sure is. It's different from what you usually hear, isn't it? New Big Whitey is the one who takes off."

"Now wait a minute, Jake."

"I'm sorry. It ain't your fault. I guess I just get mad thinkin' about it."

"Well, that doesn't give you an excuse to take things out on me. Look. Let's not let these things mess up our friendship. We're just two guys working on a project. Let's forget everything else."

Jake shook his head. "Ah, Davis. You always think you can make things work out real quick. I could tell that about you right away. You think you can make things work out just by puttin' the pieces together."

Greg looked at the boy, a little stunned.

"Now we're different," Jake went on. "No use trying to pretend we're not. And after a while you won't want to forget things. You don't want to forget you're different like they tell you you should. You want to stick around stubborn, like a wart, just the way you are, whatever you are. You don't want to forget anything."

Greg looked at Jake without having a word to say. He still felt a little shocked. At first he thought it might be his pride. He had never had trouble making a friend out of somebody if he wanted to; then he realized that the closing door had touched his heart, too.

Jake must have seen the confusion in his eyes. He softened and tried to explain further. "You don't want to sell out . . . your own. See?" he said, almost regretfully.

Greg nodded. He had always enjoyed challenges with people. But he didn't know what to do with a mass, faceless "your own." It was so final.

"Now we'd better get down to business," said Jake, and he walked over to a high enamel cupboard, opened it, and revealed several uniform boxes on every shelf. "I moved all my

61

stuff in here the other day and all Aunt Sallie's food and dishes out. Oo-EE! You should have seen her. She still forgets and goes in here to set stuff. Heh-heh!"

"Does she work a night shift?"

"Yeah. She cleans offices at the warehouse down the street."

"Hmm."

"She's a tough honey. She used to work during the day as a domestic. But she said the people who owned the house used to ring a bell for her, and nobody ever again—least of all white folks—was ever gonna ring a bell at her again, even if she had to work nights when they was sleepin'. So that's what she does." Jake walked over with a stack of four boxes. There were still many more in the cupboard.

"Jeez, Jake. I thought . . . a couple of jars or something, but nothing like this. It must have taken years."

"Naw. Only a couple of summers if you half try. Let's look at some beetles. I have more of them than anything."

"Where did you get the money for all the equipment?"

"Call this equipment? This is all junk from around the house. Look here—cardboard, some cheap tape, alcohol. These are old drawers boxes from a men's store. Only thing I ever spent money on was a cheap magnifying glass."

"Where did you learn to do all this?" Greg examined the even, carefully-labelled rows of multifarious beetles.

"There's nothing to it. One time when I was on this kick Aunt Lizbeth came in town. She asked me what I wanted and she bought me some gym shoes and a handbook on collecting."

"Hey, look. You lost a label here. I can't find it in the box anywhere, either."

"Oh. It's not lost. That's Little Red. I never identified him. I left a space to remind me. I still have piles of stuff written on him because I couldn't find him in the books. It was fun watching him and finding things out all by myself. Then he went and died." Jake shrugged his shoulders. "Guess Miss Hyde would know what he was."

"It looks like an awfully fancy collection."

"Actually it's not a big collection. It ain't even a good sample. I may have to limit my entry to beetles, if I enter. I figure I can sort them out into different groups like workers, fighters—something like that. Make drawings of the important parts, the parts that make each one special. What you laughing at?"

"I can just see you running around the fields with a butterfly net."

"Aw, come on."

"Did you ever do that, Jake?"

"No. That's why I don't have but a few butterflies that I caught with my hands. I did mean to make myself a net at one time, but then I lost interest. I was getting older and all."

"Is your beetle collection complete?"

Jake smiled. "No insect collection is ever complete. You never know what you might find. But beetles are the easiest to turn up."

"Where did you get these?"

"I told you. I started in the cellar on Langley Avenue. I'm not kidding. Then I did a lot of good hunting at the dump lot on Rydberg Avenue. Then a couple times I went swimming at the lake with Danny and his friends and I caught some on the shore." Jake thought for a while. "Do you really think I could enter a part collection, like just the beetles?"

"Oh, I couldn't tell you that. You'd have to ask that biology teacher. But it sounds okay to me, especially if you make those diagrams and write up good legends and explanations. . . ."

"Me? Write? You know I can't do English."

"I can help you with that. You write up what you want to say, and I'll help you rewrite it."

"Maybe they'd call that too much help."

"I don't see why they should. This isn't an essay contest. And it's not like I'm correcting the scientific material. But ask your teacher to be sure."

63

"All right."

"I guess . . . you don't have a typewriter."

"Nope. But I think I can get my girl Jan Spears to do some typing for me."

"Good. How about books?"

"Just the two I told you about."

"No sweat. We can go to the big library downtown. Hey, I have an idea. As long as we're going there, we can look at the collections at the museum, too. It's right there. We'll make a day of it."

"You too?"

"Sure. I like to browse around. But I can't make it tomorrow. We have a basketball game."

"With who?"

"Marlow."

"Marlow. Marlow," said Jake, snapping his fingers. "Didn't they win the playoff from the north last year?"

"That's right."

"Man, you cats up at Burnside do everything big."

"We're tough," said Greg, thumping his chest. "How about Sunday? Do you want to go downtown on Sunday?"

"I . . . uh . . . I'm not sure where the place is."

"You don't know where the museum is? Well, I'll meet you downtown. How about Advance and Fifth? Where Bogg's is?"

"I know where that is."

They looked at Jake's beetle collection some more while Jake told Greg unusual stories about some of the specimens. Soon it was time for Greg to catch the Cole Avenue bus and head for home.

He arrived home just before eleven and found both his parents still awake. "Greg, were you on Rydberg Avenue again?" his mother asked.

"No, Mom. I spent all the time at Jake's."

"Rich Wallace called."

"Yes, he was supposed to tell me about a ride. Did you tell him where I was?"

"Yes. I told him you were visiting a friend and he asked who. He thought you'd be at Virginia's. He said something about not being tired tomorrow, so you'd better go to bed. He's picking you up at eight-thirty."

"Eight-thirty? What the heck for? Sometimes Wallace thinks he's a nursemaid, telling everybody what time to go to bed and what time to get up. I know it's a bit of a ride to get there, but eight-thirty? What a fanatic!"

———✦———

"Rich was sure mad about losing that game."

"Everybody felt bad."

"But you know how Rich is."

"Yeah, a real nut." Greg and Virginia were walking to the parking lot after witnessing a double spectacle at the Burnside Heights Palace. "He just can't stand to lose," said Greg. "You'd think we'd played some second-rate team the way he expected to run off with the game."

"But Mona said he said they lost three of their seniors where we had only lost two and that we shouldn't have lost by so much."

Greg sighed. "All right. So there were a couple of mistakes. But we didn't get whipped that badly. And it was a good game, don't you think so? Besides, it's only an exhibition game. If we do as well as we should, we'll have another crack at them later on." They reached the car and Greg opened the door for Virginia. Then he walked around and slid behind the wheel.

"Rich said something about the fellows not being in shape. He said they weren't following the rules. You . . . you were out late last night, weren't you, Greg?"

"Now wait a minute. I was in great shape at the game and I never played better. I had almost eight hours of sleep, even though I didn't expect Rich to get up with the milkman to get there," Greg grumbled as he started the car. "If you ask me, Rich himself was dragging it a little."

"Mona knew you were loafing around Cole with that colored boy again."

"You were the only one I told. How did she find out?"

"I don't know."

"Oh . . . Rich knew. He called last night and my mother told him. The only thing wrong with that story is that I wasn't loafing."

"What were you doing?"

"I told you. We were looking at the insect collection he might enter in the science fair."

Virginia sighed. "I still don't see why it has to be you."

"Why not me? It's my microscope and I pushed him into it. And who else does he have?"

Virginia rolled her eyes upwards. "Just because your father is a social worker, and just because you work at a colored recreation center doesn't mean you have to be a . . . a tutor or crusader or something."

"A crusader? Is that what I look like?"

"Yes. What are you laughing at?"

"At you. At all of you, the way you all stopped what you're doing to mind my business. I must be a pretty important person. And none of you know what's going on. It's like . . . like I'm knocking my brains out to write a paper on the reproductive habits of beetles and someone comes along and says I'm writing dirty stories."

"Oh, come on, Greg," Virginia said irritably.

"Well, it's true. I didn't know I looked like a crusader. Heck. I consider Jake an equal. He's. . . ."

"Then what else is it?"

"Look. I don't know what the big deal is. I met this guy at the park; I like him because he's . . . smart, funny . . . sensitive. Sensitive—that's it. None of you knuckleheads know him but you're so worried about him. He's going to enter the Mansfield Science Fair, I lent him some stuff, and he's interested in what I have to say about his project."

"Well, how long is this going to go on?"

Greg was speechless. There was a red light and he turned

and stared at Virginia as though she were a stranger. This couldn't be Virginia demanding, assuming. . . . Someone honked the horn at him. He pushed the shift up into second and it protested with a loud "Grumph!" As they rolled along Greg groped for words. "What do you mean, 'how long'? I wasn't planning to end this friendship at the end of the fair, Virginia."

"Friendship?"

"Yes, it's a friendship." Greg stiffened all over; his foot pressed the gas pedal and the car shot down the avenue. "Furthermore, I don't see what business it is of yours or anyone else's, and I'm getting tired of hearing you ask me about it like . . . like I'm doing something wrong."

"Oh, that temper of yours. You always have to get nasty."

"Frankly, Virginia, you have a lot of nerve giving me the third degree like this."

"What do you mean?" Virginia piped.

"I don't know how to put it, Virginia, but you're getting pretty bossy about my personal affairs. Especially about this thing. I told you once before, I'll pick my own friends."

"Is he really your friend, Greg?"

"Well . . . yes," said Greg. "Sure he is. He's a new one, not a long time pal or anything like that, but . . . yes . . . he's a friend, he has the things I like in a person." Greg felt satisfied with the conclusion he had just made. "What else is a friend? He has the things I pick my friends for."

"I don't know, Greg. I just don't know."

"Aw, honey." Greg reached over and took the girl's hand. "What's bothering you? Tell me. I won't be mean, I promise. I guess I am a sorehead sometimes. But I don't know what came over you, bossing like that. It just wasn't like you, Virginia. You've never been that way before."

"Oh, Greg . . . I . . . I don't know. I suppose this colored boy is all right. If you like him, he must be. And I don't really have anything against Negroes. I'm not like that. I wouldn't want to hurt anybody, or keep him from having what he's entitled to. But . . . be friends? I couldn't. I mean

. . . none of the kids would. I mean, they have their own people and their own ways. You have plenty of friends. Really, Greg. I don't see why you have to put on this big show."

"I'm not putting on a show!"

"That's not what I mean. I mean, why do you have to associate with him, when you have so many of your own friends?"

"I'm starting to wonder if they are. Anyway, it's for you to answer, Virginia. Why shouldn't I associate with him?"

"Oh, I don't know."

"You can't just say 'I don't know'! Look what's going on in our country right now. You'd better start thinking about it. And everybody else, too."

"I know. I know." She pouted. Then after a little while, she said, "Why should I? It's not my problem. I'm not hurting anybody, so why should I go out looking for problems like you do."

"I'm not looking for problems. He's a human being."

"Oh, do what you want. I don't care. If the kids keep asking me questions, I'll tell them to go ask you. Now let's not talk about it anymore."

But Greg kept thinking about it as they rode silently through town. They arrived at Virginia's house and Greg stopped the car but made no effort to get out. He gazed blindly out of the window. She didn't know; she didn't know why. Just like that. Murders, beatings, wreckage and heartbreak. Why? Did anybody know why? A curious thought struck him. Maybe—like Virginia, who really meant no harm—nobody had ever really tried to understand why. He wondered.

Greg took a long, hard look at old Cole Rec as he rode by it, as if to reinforce the fact that he was out for an afternoon of pleasure instead of going to work. When he arrived at the meeting place, Jake was already there. They began walking up Advance Avenue, an architectural potpourri that was the cultural center of the city.

"Isn't that the library?" Jake asked as they walked by one of the buildings.

Greg looked up at him. "Yes. I thought it would be best if we went to the museum first. Don't you?"

"Suits me. What's that?"

"The music hall," Greg answered, surprised. "When was the last time you were here, Jake?"

Jake's brown face looked flushed. "I'm not sure. I think it was the sixth grade. It was a class tour."

"The sixth grade? You mean you haven't been here since?"

Jake shook his head.

"Why not?" For the kids at Burnside, the center, especially the library, was a favorite Saturday afternoon meeting place.

"No more trips."

"Well, we haven't had any tours either. Do you have to be escorted?"

"Look. You forget I'm not from Burnside."

"Well, why do you think they took you there in the first place?"

"Cause the Board of Education said to," Jake snapped.

Greg wanted to be just as snappy, but nothing came to his lips fast enough. Then he was glad it hadn't, for the last thing he wanted to do was to hurt or embarrass Jake. "They wanted to introduce you to the place," he said softly.

"Look. I know all about it. Up there in Burnside they teach you that if you take somebody to the . . . the concert or the museum, then unless he's an ape he's gonna see the finer things in life and they'll strike him like a revelation and he'll go back for more. But everybody knows the colored people are different. You don't expect them. . . ."

"Stop it!"

"It just ain't that simple, fella."

"I don't get it. I just don't get it. For a while you're all right, then—bang! I say one word and you're off, complain-

69

ing and feeling sorry for yourself." Greg spoke timidly now, afraid of making Jake angry. But to his surprise he found Jake looking troubled and . . . it looked like he was interested. Greg felt bolder. "Yes, feeling sorry for yourself," Greg went on. "Maybe *you* don't come down here, or Lester, or 'Jim Dandy' Forman, but I've seen plenty of Negroes around here, and nobody ever thinks twice about it. So there."

Jake was silent.

"Look, Jake. I'm sorry."

"No need to be. Maybe you got something there. Maybe you got something there."

"I can't figure you out, Jake. You're not dumb, and you don't seem like a sheep. You just don't seem like the kind of guy who would follow everybody else when you knew they were being stupid. You seem independent. But now you're telling me. . . ."

"It ain't so much just followin' everybody. It's . . . it's like eatin' chitt'lins."

"What do you mean?"

"I said it's like eatin' chitt'lins. Ever eat chitt'lins?"

"No. And to tell you the truth, I don't even know what they are except that they're something to eat. What's the point?"

"Well, people from my part of town eat chitt'lins; people from yours don't. Now, there ain't really nothing right or wrong about eatin' chitt'lins; you just either eat 'em or you don't. Likewise, at your school the kids read books and come down to the library; down here we groove. You dig it?"

"Hmm . . . go on."

"Now, nobody ever came out and *said* that libraries and museums were for squares or anything like that. They just don't say anything about it, period. Libraries and concerts are what book people go to, that's all. You take your school tour of where book people go and get a day off from school and forget it."

"Chitt'lins, schmittlins. Maybe so. But you still sound like you ought to know better, Jake."

70

"Well . . . that's now."

"Better late than never. Anyway, you'd better start hanging around these square digs if you expect to enter the science fair."

"I will. Don't worry."

"By the way, Jake. What are chitt'lins?"

"Hog's maw." They strolled past another ornate building. "All right, teacher," said Jake, "as long as you're cluein' me in on the cultured things today, you can tell me what this is, too."

"The art museum."

"Jeez! Which one of these places is the museum? The one with the collections?"

"The one right here on the corner. Say, Jake. Why didn't you ever look for Little Red at your library. You probably would've found him there."

"Ain't no library in Cole."

"Jake. . . ."

"Uh-huh?"

"You ought to at least try to do something about the way you talk. Sometimes it sounds terrible."

"I guess maybe you're right. I'm getting a little tired of the bag myself, now that I have other things on my mind. You just keep after me."

"All right. It'll be a deal."

"Whenever I talk jive talk, you punch me out."

"All right." It would be an insurmountable task, Greg thought, the way Jake could go on. "Well, here we are."

They walked up the wide marble steps and into the Mansfield Municipal Museum. Jake turned his head in all directions, his eyes large with curiosity. Greg went over to the directory and heard Jake whispering behind him: "Hall of

"We didn't come here for that, Jake. And I don't think we can squeeze it in. You can come back some other time."

"I'm gonna do that. Hey. There's a lot of people here."
Mammals . . . Prehistoric Life . . . Dinosaur Hall . . . Hey, let's look at that."

71

"Sure. It's Sunday afternoon."

They looked at the directory again. "Well, here it is," said Jake. "Insects. Third floor. South Wing East. Hall D. Man! You know where all that is?"

"I know enough about this place to be able to find it," Greg said confidently. He usually spent his time on the civilizations floor, especially in the ancient Greek section. Once in a while he would look at prehistoric life.

The natural history floor was radiant in glossy white stone, and Jake looked around and peered into doorways as they passed—Hall of Mammals, Reptiles, Arthropods—reluctantly following Greg's brisker pace. "A pretty crazy pad for fossils," he said.

"Do you have any spiders?" Greg asked as they passed by the arthropods.

"A few. Why? Do you? I'll ask Aunt Sal what she uses on them."

Greg laughed.

"Yeah, I do," said Jake.

The boys spent an hour in the dark insect hall. Jake looked at the displays and studied the constructions of enlarged models; Greg glanced cursorily at the exhibits and read a few legends. He began to get giddy, dance around and make imaginary basketball shots. "Hey, Jake," he called.

"Yeah?"

"You ought to have a collection called 'Household Pests'. Then you could put the spiders in, too."

"I could even dig up some rats for that. Might even stick in some people I know, too."

"Yeah. I know some people I'd like to stick in a box, too. I can just see them now, sitting in there and looking out and wondering what it was all about. Uh . . . Got any ideas yet, Jake. I'm starting to feel itchy."

"Yeah. I notice you're crackin' up." Jake scratched the back of his head. "Yeah. I got a few ideas. I'm gonna try to make up my mind about a few things tonight so I can have

72

something to discuss with Miss Hyde tomorrow. Do you want to leave now?"

"I just thought we could use a change of scenery. But I don't want to rush you. You take your time."

"It's okay. I looked real good. Where do you want to go?"

"You want to look at the mummies? Or those dinosaurs?"

"Crazy."

"You really go for this biology bit, don't you?" Greg said to Jake as they made their way downstairs.

Jake just shrugged his shoulders.

"What do you think you'll do with it?"

"What do you mean, 'do'?"

"Your plans for the future. Do you think you'll work in biology or science?"

"How should I know?"

It was a dead stop, but as so many times before, Greg knew he had to go on before silence killed any ideas he wanted to plant in Jake's mind. "Well . . . you seem to like science more than other things"—he tried to sound casual—"so I just wondered if you ever thought of being a biologist or something."

"You don't think of being something," Jake said.

"Why not?"

"Aw, what's the sense. . . ."

"Come on, Jake. Do you think you'd like to work in biology?"

"Look. Just because I didn't have anything better to do than mess around rubbish barrels when I was a kid doesn't mean I want to spend the rest of my life doin' it—if what I want to do has anything to do with anything in the first place. 'Entomologists'—that's what they call them. Insect collectors."

"Well, there are other things. You once mentioned working in a lab. You know, wearing a white coat, examining things under a microscope—stuff like that."

"That sounds nice. But maybe I'll be too busy being president of the United States."

"Uh . . . you have a way with people. You could always be a doctor."

Jake turned a bit serious. "Me?"

"Why not?"

"Well, I don't think I'm the doctor type, but. . . ."

"Yes?"

"That other thing. The white coat bag. That kind of medicine man. Maybe I'd like to work behind the scene, with diseases and stuff."

"There!"

For what might have been the first time in his life, Jake fancied possibilities for himself. But familiar obstacles reminded him of the difficulties. "How could a black boy like me ever go to college and medical school on top of that?"

"Jake, we've been all over that."

"I don't know why you start talking like this. How can you, an ofay from Burnside, really know what it's like to be a colored boy from Cole?"

Greg couldn't argue with that. Maybe he shouldn't be opening his mouth, he thought, about things he might not really understand. But silence was a sign of defeat, and he couldn't admit that to Jake. It might be contagious. "I agree that it's a tough world, Jake. You might even have to borrow money, or wait for a while and work. And you'd certainly have to do well in school."

"Work. Hmph. To work you need a job."

"I told you, there are special sources just for Negroes."

"Aunt Sallie says all this stuff about helping the black people is a bunch of junk to keep them dumb, happy and quiet."

"Jake, what can I say when you talk like that? It's her way of seeing things, that's all. If you want to look at it her way too, what can anybody say? I don't have anything against your aunt, but it seems to me that every time you come off with one of those hard luck stories of yours, it's 'Aunt Sallie said'. What makes you think she knows it all? Why don't you stop listening to her like she's the last word? Maybe you

74

ought to stop listening to Lester and Forman, too. Talk to someone who's not so sour on everything. Talk to someone who knows what he's talking about."

"Like who? Like the counselor at school who doesn't even want to see us? Like the teachers who hate us?"

"That's a bunch of baloney. Your biology teacher's all right, isn't she?"

"Yeah. . . ."

"And as for that counselor, put him to work. Go to the library once in a while. To the counseling division there. The place is loaded with scholarship and loan information. And with poor, underprivileged Negroes like poor-soul Jake Williams," Greg added with a cautious sarcasm. "Only they're getting it all while you're crying in your coke and makin' the scene. Of course, you've gotta have the stuff. And nobody's gonna come begging for you. . . ."

He had hit Jake in the ego where it hurt. "I do have the stuff. I do!" the colored boy snapped. "Shoot! I'm gonna get me some of that gravy, too. I'm gon' do it. I'm gon' start right in now. I'm gon' go down to that counselor's office and say, "Meers, baby, I think you got something of mine. . . .""

CONFLICT

The Burnside varsity, red, wet, gasping for breath, dropped to the floor by the bench. Frank Klinglehaus lay flat on his back and moaned "Ooooo . . . That was as bad as a game." The clock in the gym said twenty to six. They had been scrimmaging since four o'clock. Rich Wallace sat on the bench leaning on his elbows, his chin jammed into his cupped hands, gazing sadly at the floor. But the tenseness of his body showed that he still had more energy than his depleted teammates. All the boys had finally assembled. They waited. But Rich was still deep in his own thoughts.

He started to bob his head up and down, lips tight, and finally muttered, "You guys tired, huh?" The boys moaned. "Creampuffs," he said. "You haven't seen anything yet. Henry and McKing went to see Bedford play Friday. Maybe you heard. They creamed Goldsmith. That's right. The eastern contenders for state championship last year. Know why? Those black boys are tough, that's why." Greg hoped he wouldn't mouth off too long. But he went on. "They ran the legs off Goldsmith. Not even one substitution, because they don't have too much on the bench. And they didn't even take one time out, either. No sir. Blackies are something else. Goldsmith couldn't even find the ball half the time." The boys listened, their minds emptied of all else from exhaustion, their eyes watery and glittering in a rosy sea of flushed faces.

Rich went on without any interruptions. "But I'm not worrying about Goldsmith. I'm worrying about the Burnside Bats. And we'd better not lose this game Friday. We should never have flubbed that first game, and we'd better not lose this one. Especially to a bunch of. . . ."

Greg shivered. Rich kept it up. Greg choked up as though the contents of his stomach had been forced up and he tried to swallow as Rich went on with an ugly tirade of name calling. A picture of Jake's dark face with its large, soft brown eyes wandered into his mind. This is silly, he thought. Wallace didn't even know Jake. He wondered if Rich knew any Negroes. A Negro might be just an idea to him. How could you call an idea a dirty name? Still the painful picture was there—Jake, standing in the center of a crowded room, glancing around shyly with questioning eyes, unaware that in their foreign tongue the people ridiculed and insulted him. Greg wanted to run up and grab Rich and tell him to shut up.

Painfully, his attention drifted back to Rich's harangue. "And do you know why we were slow?" he was saying. "Because we're out of shape, that's why. Nobody cares. Everybody's soft. Nobody wants to follow the rules. Everybody wants to have a good time. Danny's out with this girl, Frankie's I don't know where, Davis is down at the Darktown Strutter's Ball. . . ."

Greg jolted. He stared at Rich. Could anybody have that much nerve? Greg saw Rich's mouth moving; he saw some of the boys grinning; he saw some of them shifting nervously on the floor; but he heard nothing. It was as though somebody had turned the sound off on a television program. Greg stared and stared. Yes. Rich had really said it. Greg looked around at the other boys, flushed, disturbed, but making no protests. Chickens. Well, he had had enough of Rich. Rich wasn't going to get away with that in front of all the boys. He rose.

Rich stopped talking and looked back. The others turned. "Something the matter, Davis?"

"Yeah. You, Wallace. And your filthy mouth. You'd better learn to mind your own business." The boys on the floor were paralyzed.

"This heah ball team is mah business, ho-NEY," Rich sneered. A couple of the boys sniggered, but most of them just stared. "Anythin' else on yo' mind, baby?"

"Yeah. I was in perfect shape for that game Saturday, and you know I was." Greg paused, then spoke with dead softness. "Now, I don't want to hear you make one more dirty crack about where I go. Do you hear?"

"Am ah tellin' you where to go, baby?" Rich squealed. "All ah'm sayin' is, you can't play a good game of ball when you been doin' the mess around the night befo'."

"Oh, Lord!"

"I don't really care where you have your kicks, Davis. Most of us are gonna cruise around Bedford ourselves after the game, aren't we, fellas? After we whitewash those boys" —a few teammates tittered appreciatively at the pun— "we're gonna ride around and look over the town. Wanna be the guide, Davis?"

"You rotten. . . ." Greg wheeled around and stormed from the gym. There was no sound behind him now. As he neared the exit, he blankly noticed that McKing had come in and was standing just inside the doorway. He brushed by Mc-King silently and ploughed through the doors leading to the lockers. Thoughts began to find their way back into his mind. "They oughta beat us good," he thought.

———✦———

Greg frowned. There was one more period yet. He was gathering up some sweaty, grimy gym clothes that had tumbled out of his locker when he went for his books. Right now he wished he could take everything out of the locker and just disappear for a while. At least for this week. After yesterday's notoriety he wondered how he could make it through the next four days in one piece. Friday was that Bedford game; Saturday was Rich's sister's big Hallowe'en party. He could never fink out on that; Virginia had been making costumes for weeks. Bad timing, Davis, he thought to himself. He had picked the wrong time to have it out with the captain. Too bad. But what else could he have done?

Maybe it hadn't been as bad as he thought. Maybe everyone had forgotten the whole thing. Maybe nobody even knew about it except the boys. But that was too much to hope for. It was like a battle between two giants. "The battle of the giants." That was what the big poster had read at the last drive-in feature he and Virginia had seen, "King Kong vs. Godzilla." Both he and Wallace were fire-breathers in this battle. He sighed. Some of the kids had looked at him strangely today; only Virginia had the gall to ask him about it. Well, there was no sense in fretting about it. You just had to wait these things out.

Just then he noticed fat Henry Johnson charging up to him. Fat Henry had one chunky finger raised, signaling Greg to wait. Did he have a message from Rich, Greg wondered, or did he want help in trig again? Henry was too shy to ask the real brains for help; besides, he knew him from basketball. Although he had hoped to spend the period alone, Greg admitted to Henry that he had some spare time and they walked into homeroom together.

They sat down in the back of the room and Greg opened his textbook to "Trigonometric Functions." All the while Henry stared at Greg dumbly and expectantly, circling his tongue over his lips and not saying a word. Something was really on Henry's mind, and it wasn't trig. Henry kept staring nervously. Greg pretended not to notice. He peered intently at the beginning of the chapter and tried to puzzle out

Henry's expression. It sure was a queer one. Henry was obviously curious about something.

"Uh . . . was there any special problem you wanted to know about or just the whole idea in general?" Greg asked. Henry reddened. "Henry? What did you want to know?"

"Hey . . . uh . . . what's he like? That colored kid you loaf with?"

So that's it, Greg thought. He might have known. He wished he had something devastating to say to Henry. He would have loved to blast him with something. Instead he took a deep breath, leaned back, clasped his hands behind his head, and looked up. Henry blushed and shifted in his seat. Greg was pleased. Let Henry sweat it out.

Then it suddenly seemed vain and silly. Henry's question had been innocent enough. He had gotten awfully edgy again, Greg thought; too defensive about the whole thing. He looked up at Henry's round pink face. Why give old Henry a rough time? Was it his fault he had never met a Negro up there in East Burnside? Besides, what good would it do Jake? What good would it do anybody to play this silly game?

"Well," Greg finally began, "Jake is one of the nicest guys I ever met."

"What makes you think that?"

"Well, he's . . . funny. And he's . . . honest. He's not afraid to let you know what makes him scared. It sort of gives you the feeling that he's a real human being." Greg had never thought of these things just this way before, until now when he tried to tell someone else. "You know, when you meet someone like that, you get the feeling that you can say what makes you scared and mad, too. You don't have to play the role. Know what I mean?"

Henry didn't. Furthermore he looked puzzled and unsatisfied. "Does he go to school?"

"Yes. He's a junior like us."

"What's he do for kicks?"

"He plays basketball, likes to dance, likes to run his mouth. He's really funny."

"Where does he play ball? For Cole?"

"No. For one of the public teams called the Blackhawks."

"Couldn't he qualify for athletics?"

"Yes. He's very smart, in fact. He gets A's and B's in the sciences, and he's entering. . . ."

"That's Cole High School."

"Maybe," Greg mumbled. "Still, I hear more sense coming from his mouth sometimes than I do from half of the jerks around this place."

"I'll bet he's a lot of laughs, huh?"

"He's comic sometimes, yeah. But he has his serious. . . ."

"Negroes are natural comedians."

"Glad to have your opinion on the matter, Henry," said Greg, slapping his desk. "Is there anything else you want to tell me?"

"Yeah. Bedford's center is six feet-six. They call him 'Daddy Longlegs'. Bi-i-ig Daddy Longlegs," Henry repeated with a mock southern accent. "How big is your boy?"

Greg peered into Henry's eyes. "He's nine feet-ten. And he's as fat as you. He pushes goof balls, sniffs glue, mugs old ladies and burns watermelons on people's lawns. And if he caught you, he'd boil you and eat you alive. Now beat it, Henry. You're wasting my time."

Henry stood up. "You'd better watch it, Davis." He shoved his glasses up his nose, pushed his belly under his belt and walked away.

———⌀———

"Well," said Coach McKing, slapping his thigh, "you saw what they got up there." It was twenty minutes before game time, and the Burnside players had just come down from a short workout in the gym. "The center—Daddy Longlegs they call him—isn't real fast," McKing went on, "but when

81

you're six feet-six that makes up for it. Danny, you ought to be able to cover him by leaping at the right time. At the right time. Don't wear yourself out. Number seven, 'Roach' Ellston, is the one you've been hearing about. He's the fastest thing this state has seen for a long time and he's full of tricks. You cover 'im, Rich. He does a lot of faking and pivoting, so watch those fouls. Keep your eye on the ball all the time but don't jump at every move he makes. And don't crowd him. Use your brains more, your feet less. Another thing: he does a lot of shooting from the outside, so don't let him jam you under the board.

"Same goes for you, Greg. You've got Hawkins, number nine, and he's pretty good on the jump shots. Frank, Carl, the guards are good. Furman can jump. He can cop a shot right out of the air. And Stokes, number fourteen, will knock the ball from you and you'll go on dribbling air. They do some nice shooting to boot. Furman does some nice set shots. So watch that dribbling and do some passing. But careful passing.

"You guys are gonna be pretty busy at the board with Furman and Longlegs around so don't all crowd up there, hear me? That's about all I can think of now, so relax. Talk over your plays and go out and take some long lazy shots and limber up. No showing off up there, d'ya hear? Because these guys are gonna run your buckets off. Okay. Now git."

The Bats thumped up the steps from the locker room. It was 7:18—twelve minutes till game time. "Ya-ay!" came a roar from the Burnside rooting section, along with stomping, whistling and clapping. About five hundred rooters had made the trip to Bedford to cheer the Bats. Mona Wallace, dressed in a blue satin skirt and white sweater, led the rooting section in a cheer, kicking briskly and punching the air. "Beat-Beat-Beat 'em, Bats! Beat-Beat-Beat 'em, Bats!"

The Bedford Beetles were working out by the other board. Jimmy Stokes was feeding the ball to the Beetle line in front of the home team stands. "Hup!" he'd grunt as he shot the ball to a running teammate; "Hey-e-ey" he groaned as the boy scooted up and shot. "Hup! . . . He-e-ey. . . . Hup! . . . He-e-ey . . . Hup!" he sang, and the Bedford line swung around rhythmically from the banking board to the back. "These coloreds always know how to put on a show, huh?" Carl murmured to Frank as the Bats looked on for a few seconds.

The Bedford fans were a dark sea of waves that surged, broke with a handclap, and surged back as they sang "Ah, scoo-bi-dy scoo, Ah, scoo-bi-dy scoo, Ah, scoo-bi-dy scoo, Ah. . . ." Two cheerleaders, a dark boy and girl in bright orange satin, did the Mashed Potatoes to the chant. Greg was enjoying the show, but Rich Wallace tapped him on the shoulder and said, "Let's go, Davis. This isn't Cole Rec." And they trotted over for some shots.

The timekeeper and scorekeeper took their places and the referees came in with the balls. Seven twenty-five. The Bats had formed two lines. Someone shot, retrieved his own ball, and fed it to the opposite line. Greg heard Rich say, "No black boy's gonna run my bucket off." Greg turned around. Rich was looking at Roach Ellston. Roach was standing by the Bedford rooters, joggling his head to the chant and swaying. He had hard narrow eyes and was short and thickly built for a basketball player.

The referee blew his whistle and the teams jogged over to their benches. The Bats formed a circle, extended their hands and Rich began rattling their customary short prayer: "All right, let's get 'em!" yelled Rich. The starting five went out in the court. The referee came to the center circle and blew the whistle.

"Daddy Longlegs," clap! "Daddy Longlegs," clap! "Daddy. . . ."

The referee held up the ball like a turkey on a platter; Danny and Daddy Longlegs crouched down. Another whistle. Up popped the ball. It was a long moment—then it was all over. Longlegs rose effortlessly above Danny like a black

83

eel, his long fingers tipped the ball to Jimmy Stokes. Stokes broke from Carl and snatched it like a frog's tongue darting at a fly. Rich hissed.

The Bats were completely taken by surprise. The Beetles were incredibly fast and the Bats made the mistake of trying to guard every little movement and were left behind. In no time it was 2-0, 4-0, 6-0, 8-0, and the Bats were paralyzed with confusion. Greg's man made a jump shot, bringing it up to 10-0, and Rich took the ball out.

Over to Greg; back to Rich; they worked it down the floor. They tried to set Frank up, but Roach Ellston intercepted the ball. Ellston faked, pivoted, dribbled; the whistle screamed. Foul! A foul called against Rich. "He charged!" Rich said, but the referee looked at him sternly as he wordlessly shook his head. You didn't often hear a player say anything to a ref, but Rich was out of his mind; no doubt about that. His face was red and his hair hung over his brow in a wild way.

Ellston was shifting around in the keyhole. Greg heaved and sweat clouded his eyes. But under the glare of the lights and through the stinging sweat he saw Ellston sink the ball to make the score 11-0.

The Bats worked it down again. Over to Carl. Carl faked, dribbled, faked again and shot. Greg gasped. The Burnside fans moaned. Stokes had leaped and slammed the ball down. Rich and Longlegs scrambled for it. "Black. . . ." Greg heard Rich gasp. He had lost all his cool and the hate was coming out. The whistle. Jump ball. Oh, man, forget it; the giant was jumping. Longlegs tipped the ball to Hawkins and with some passing Furman sank it from the outside, 13-0. The Negro fans were singing. "Time. Time, Rich," Frank gasped. Rich just ignored him and took the ball out.

Three minutes to go in the first quarter. Rich and Greg worked it up the floor. Rich to Carl; Carl dribbled, pivoted, dribbled some more—just couldn't get away from Stokes, who had hands there, everywhere, like an octopus. The Burnside fans were panicky. "Shoot! Shoot, Frank! Shoot!"

they shouted. Frank waved the ball in confusion. "Shoot! Shoot!" Frank sprang for a jump shot. It hit the board, rattled between the board and the rim of the basket, and barely made it through. 13-2. The Burnside fans screamed and began to clap. "Let's-go-Burn-side-We-want-some ac-tion! Let's-go-Burn-side-We-want-some ac-tion! Let's go. . . ." The whistle screeched. Time out for Burnside.

The Bats trudged over to the bench. McKing opened his arms to gather them in a circle. They crouched down, all soaked and blinded by sweat.

"Oh, man, Coach. Oh, man."

"They're really fast," said Frank, shaking his head.

"They got us, all right."

"Shut up, all of you," grumbled Rich. "We haven't lost yet and those black boys aren't gonna beat us, either. We just have to start plugging the basket like that last one. . . . 13-2. Cripes! We've gotta score!"

"Now wait a minute, Wallace," said McKing. "I'm running this show. Forget about baskets now. Forget about what those kids are shouting out there. I want you guys to cool it. D'ya hear me? You guys are all shook up and worn out."

"They got a couple of thousand years practice from swingin' on trees. . . ."

"Shut up, Wallace. I'm talkin' now. You all missed chargin' plenty of times. I want you to go out there and pass it around, slow down, cool down, keep your eyes open for a while and your heads clear till you get to know what you're up against. Watch 'em. D'ya hear me? And after you know 'em a little better, then aim for the bucket. All right. Less 'n two minutes to go. Remember what I said."

They did. And in a few minutes the Bats were able to get a little control of things. Ellston played around and tried to shoot, but Rich stopped him dead and Ellston momentarily lost balance. "That's all, black boy," Rich muttered. Ellston glared. Greg hoped Rich would cool off; he was making everyone nervous. Ellston pitched it underhand to Hawkins. Greg stepped back to watch him better. He tried to calm down. McKing was right. You had to keep your wits. These guys would confuse you if you panicked at every move. They were full of tricks. Now Hawkins paused, facing the basket; Greg crouched. In a split second they were both up. . . . Smack! Got it! thought Greg. The ball slammed down. "That's showin' 'em," Rich cheered from behind.

Carl was racing down the floor with the ball. Over to Rich, to Danny, to Frank. Frank got in under . . . up . . . the ball rolled in. 13-4. The Bats fans roared. A faint buzz. A whistle. First quarter.

The teams trotted over to their benches. Everyone was tired. "How do my boys feel now?" McKing greeted them with a tired smile.

"Better. . . . " "A little better. . . ."

"There's a long way to go," said Carl.

"You're right about keeping cool, Coach," said Greg. "It really helps."

"That's for sure."

Rich Wallace looked his old cocky self. "We'll get those monkeys under control," he said.

Mona and Tony Stafford started the Burnside cheerleaders in a song and the fans joined in. "Cheer, cheer for old Burnside High. . . ."

In the second quarter the Bats held the Beetles back and edged up closer and closer to their score. And Rich and Roach Ellston had something going full steam. When Roach managed to lose Rich for a second, Rich recovered, but he was mad. "That's all, Rasmus," he said as he stayed Ellston's shot. Greg was covering Hawkins on the other side of the basket. Rich got 'im, he thought. Why did he have to open his mouth? Lucky the ref hadn't heard.

Ellston sneaked the ball over to Hawkins. "How's that, bleach job?" he said. They were liable to get in a fight right on the floor. Then what? Greg thought of the crew of Negroes behind him. Hawkins snapped an overhead pass to Longlegs.

Still the Bats held the Beetles away from the basket.

Stokes caught a pass and made a couple of bounces toward the board. But in a split second Rich swatted the ball and it tumbled near Greg. Hawkins threw himself at the ball and Greg lunged after him. Hawkins pounced on it and rolled over, holding it up. Greg fell on him. The whistle screeched. Darn! thought Greg. Couldn't stop myself there. Hawkins took his time straightening out. "Everything all right, fella?" said the referee. "Yeah," said the boy.

Greg walked to the keyhole and a shook-up Rich paused nearby. "Cripes, Davis, how could you be so clumsy?"

"Get lost, Wallace. Anybody can fall. And you'd better keep your dirty mouth shut on the floor."

"Mind your own business."

Toot! The ref glared at them. The Bedford fans were cheering. "Hawkins! Hawkins!—Hawk! Hawk! Hawkins! Hawkins!—Hawk! Hawk!" The Hawk brought it up to 16 for the Beetles. There were four minutes to go and the Bats had six baskets to catch up.

Rich was in a rage. Greg saw his lips moving and saw Stokes glare at him through angry eyes. Hateful eyes. How could Rich have the rotten nerve? What if they'd really get mad? Be good for him, Greg thought. Stokes dribbled furiously down the floor. He flipped the ball to Longlegs who effortlessly popped it, but it hit the rim and Danny tipped it away. Rich caught it and raced down the floor hollering, "Let's go!"

"Ain't goin' nowhere, cracker," called Stokes. They were getting louder.

They were at the other end of the court. Greg took a pass and scored. The board blinked, then registered 16-8. Hawkins moved it down the floor. To Longlegs. Longlegs to Stokes, Stokes to Ellston. Ellston leaped up but it hit the rim. "Too bad, Rasmus," Rich muttered. But then Longlegs tipped it in. Rich heard the roar of the Bedford crowd and turned just in time to see the ball drop out of the bottom of the net. "Eat that, boy," said Ellston.

Rich carried the ball down the floor. A minute and a half.

Rich to Danny, Danny to Frank, and Frank to Carl, who swerved around Stokes. Carl was in the clear. . . . up. . . . it didn't even brush the rim. A beautiful shot, bringing it up 18-10. It started a good streak for the Bats and they brought their score to 16. The Burnside rooters clamored for more. "Let's-go-Burnside We-want-some ac-tion! Let's-go-Burnside-We-want-some ac-tion!" The Bedford fans swayed and sang "Hold 'em back! Hold 'em back! Wa-ay back!"

Furman took the ball out and hurled it high. Longlegs caught it in the air where nobody could reach. It happened so fast, Greg was caught dragging behind. A quick pass to Hawkins, and Hawkins, barely out of Greg's reach, made a good shot. 20-16. Greg took it out and passed to a hysterical Rich Wallace; Rich raced madly down the floor. Only twenty-five seconds to go. Rich passed to Carl, barely missing Stokes's outstretched arm. Carl leaped desperately for a long shot, not even taking the time to get set. The ball just cleared the rim, stood unbelievably still for an incredibly long time, and slowly toppled in. 20-18. Screams from the Burnside fans. Bzzzp! The buzzer. Bang! The gun. Greg sighed, sweat flooding his eyes.

The boys jogged wearily down the steps. "Shoot, Davis" —Greg heard Rich's mumbling behind him—"if it wasn't for that last one you lost, it would've been a tie."

"Wha . . . ? You got a lotta nerve, Wallace. You lost more'n I did."

"But that one. We were really moving the second quarter."

"But all ten of them. Hey. And you'd better stop mouthing off with this name-calling."

"Aw, mind your own business. I don't tell you to stop loving 'em, so don't tell me to stop hating 'em."

"This is my business. I'm on this team, too. Why should we play our hearts out if you're going to blow the game with your big mouth?"

"Listen, Davis. . . ."

"Beside the fact that it's a lousy thing to do—of course, nobody expects you to worry about that—you're only risking fouls."

"The ref didn't hear me."

"I don't know why you'd say that. Everybody else did."

"Everybody's mumbling around. But you don't hear the black boys, do you? Naw, they're lily white." Rich forced a shrill giggle.

"Did anyone ever tell you you're a lousy comedian, Wallace? I didn't hear anything until you started it. And you'd better check the foul rules. I think after the first time they warn you. . . ."

"And maybe you'd better keep your mind on the game instead of listening for noises, Davis."

"How could anybody help hearing you?"

They came near to the rest of the boys, who were resting, sapped of their strength, on the benches. "Don't bother me, Davis," Rich said as they walked over. "Cool it. Save your energy. You'll need it. There's another half, remember?"

"It's a dirty way to play ball," Greg persisted, and the weary boys looked up curiously. "Trying to demoralize. . . ."

"Are you saying I play dirty, Davis?" Rich said in a loud indignant voice.

That sneak, thought Greg. He had seen it so many times. Rich would wait for just the right time, like now, when he had an audience, and blow things up and put somebody on the defensive. It made him angrier to think about it and he just stood still and boiled.

"Well? Come on, Davis," Rich demanded. "Either say it or back down." The boys waited.

"You won't hear me back down," Greg said slowly.

"What's this all about?" Carl whispered to Frank.

"I'm not sure."

Greg eyed Rich steadily, his eyes straining to keep contact with Rich's. Rich had trapped himself now. He surely wouldn't back down; yet there wasn't enough time for him to carry on the argument. McKing had just come in and was talking to Henry. Greg had the last word and with that, he stared at Rich. It was a long silence.

But Danny broke it. "Don't take it too seriously, Greg," Danny said softly. They both turned. "I don't think it really shakes those guys up. I . . . I don't think they care too much."

So. Those chicken livers had known what they were carping about, Greg thought bitterly. "Naw. Naw. They don't care," Greg mimicked. "They don't have feelings. They aren't human. . . ."

"That's the first smart thing you said all night," said Rich.

Stupid Danny, getting Rich off the hook like that. It didn't take much to put old poisonmouth back in the ring. Some teammates, sitting there waiting for a show.

"Aw, he just likes 'em," said Rich, and the boys chuckled in relief from the tension. Spineless apes, thought Greg. Now he felt like he was fighting all of them.

But something was bothering Carl. "I . . . I don't know, Rich. I wasn't gonna say anything, but maybe you'd better knock it off. I don't like the looks they've been giving you. They might . . . start something. There are a lot of Negroes here, and. . . ."

"All stupid."

"You have no right to risk trouble for all of us," said Greg. "Get your own brains knocked out if you want to. Might do you some good. But think about all the kids who came here."

"Shut up, Davis. This is Bedford. Not Watts."

"You can never tell, Rich," said Frank.

"Rich," Carl said softly, "Stokes did say something to your boy."

"Oh yeah? What he say?"

"He said . . . 'You oughta give that . . . cracker a good . . . carving.' I couldn't hear the rest. I . . . I tell you, Rich. It made me scared. Maybe they'll wait for us. . . ."

90

Rich sobered. "I didn't hear that," he said after a while. "You weren't near them."

Rich looked down and muttered to himself. McKing was finally coming over but everything had been said. "Well," he drawled, "glad to see my boys feeling better. I think you're on the ground now. Let me tell you a couple things I noticed from the bench. . . ."

Bedford made a couple of substitutions in the third quarter, but the Bats's first team stayed in. Daddy Longlegs copped the jump shot again. The Beetles worked the ball down the floor where Hawkins missed a shot. But Longlegs tipped it in. It was a fast, heavy-scoring quarter for both sides. By the time there was less than a minute to play, the score was tied at 42. Ellston fouled Rich for one shot. The players gathered around the keyhole and Rich sunk the ball to put the Bats ahead 43-42. The buzzer sounded.

When the Burnside team gathered near the bench Rich was panting but confident and said, "Well, this is it, friends. We're gonna give those boys everything we've got. Wha'dya say, Davis?"

"Huh? What do you mean, 'Davis'?"

"You were a little slow there, Davis. A couple of times I wasn't sure you'd make it down the floor. I was starting to wonder what side you're on. Your passes were sloppy and you've been chewin' the fat with Hawkins too much."

"You mind your own business."

"Aw, cripes," Carl groaned. "Why don't you two knock it off?"

"You gotta keep your eye on those black boys all the time," Rich said. "They're tough. They're something else. Ever try to catch a roach? Maybe you're a little tired, huh? Been working too hard? What do you think, Coach?"

"I'm thinkin' which one of you two guys to yank," McKing said, screwing up his right eye. "Notice I said 'two', Wallace. Now it's true that you could've tried to get a couple passes, Greg. You should know your man a little better by now. And it's true you were slow coming down the floor a couple times. But so were you, Wallace. All you guys are tired, these boys've given you the worst workout you ever had. And they've got energy you haven't even seen yet. Moxie will put his regulars back in now. Don't forget that. Before you guys start thinkin' you're hot stuff, just remember: you made all your scores last quarter on their scrubs.

"You, Carl, let a couple bounces go right past your nose without even stickin' your arm out. Danny, I think you let this Longlegs get you down. He's not too hard to figure out, you know. But you stopped trying. As for you, Wallace, I don't see how you can be doing your job with your mind on Greg so much." With that McKing threw off his controlled matter-of-factness. His face turned redder and his voice got louder. "Now I'm tellin' you, I'm sittin' here watchin' all of you. I'm the only one that can do that. It's your job to keep one eye on the ball, one on your man, one on everybody else, your mouths shut, and you'll be busy enough. Ya hear?" The boys were silent. "Keep your fights off the court and out of my life, ya hear? Now. Are you feeling okay, Greg?"

"I didn't say anything, did I? He said it," Greg snarled, jutting his chin at Rich.

"That's all I wanna know. Now git! Alla you!"

Bedford took the jump and scored to make it 44-43. Rich took it out, passed it to Frank and Frank gave it to Carl. Carl dribbled and Stokes swatted the ball. Rich swore. "Gotta learn to play the game, man," Ellston droned.

"We'll show you who can play, uncle," Rich threatened. "Where's your eyes, Carl?" The ball had gone out of bounds. Rich took it out and passed to Danny in the keyhole. Danny caught it, lunged to move in, but was stopped short. He held the ball high, but everyone was covered. The seconds ticked away while Danny looked around, helpless and confused. The Beetles were determined now. They looked tougher than Greg had seen them all night and their black eyes were radiant. The Bats were tired. Bedford had managed those substitutions, but the Burnside starting five had played all night.

Danny was really stuck. He didn't dare chance an over-head pass with Longlegs guarding him. He bounced to the side. The Burnside fans were excited. "Let's-go-Burn-side-We-want-some ac-tion!" they chanted, but not with their earlier spirit. This was the showdown, but the quarter had been a slow one and they were tired and restless. There was angry shouting above the relentless chant. "Move it! Move it!" "Pass!" C'mon, Danny!" "Pass!" "Pass!" They thumped their heels furiously on the stands. Then the whistle screeched. Danny had left it too long. He moaned. Rich glared. The Burnside fans booed.

"Jus' ain't got what it takes, man," Ellston sneered.

"This game ain't over yet," Rich snarled. The referee glanced at them both sternly.

Longlegs took the ball out of bounds and hurled it into the air. Furman leaped up, took it down and raced over toward the basket. He pitched to Ellston; Ellston weaved in and scored. 46-43, Bedford.

Rich and Greg took it down the floor. Greg was weary. The noise, the harsh lights, the heat, the sweat, making that stretch down the floor over and over again.

Greg passed to Carl. The Bats rallied and within the next few minutes they brought themselves up to a lead of 47 over 46. Three minutes to go. During the next sixty seconds there was a personal foul by Rich, scoring on both sides, and the score was tied at 49.

Greg brought the ball down the floor, his lungs burning from the stale gym air. All the boys crowded up at the basket, leaving Rich open for a set shot. The clock ticked; the ball arched high and slipped in! 51-49, Burnside.

Bedford rolled it down the floor again. To Hawkins, to Longlegs, to Ellston. Greg saw Rich hovering close over Ellston and muttering. Ellston looked angry. He arched backward painfully and swung the ball over his head from side to side, looking for a way to break out of the cage Rich had made with his arms and body. The Bedford fans were booing softly. Greg expected the ref to call a foul on Rich.

Toot! There it was. No. . . . Charging! Charging . . . ? Now the Bedford fans roared angrily and pounded on the bleachers. Another whistle. Rich had called time. The Bats jogged over to the bench. "How about that?" Frankie murmured.

Rich began babbling immediately, gasping for the words. "I say we freeze. A minute to go, and a lot can happen in that time."

"Yeah, maybe," said King. "But it's only a two point lead."

The whistle blew. Rich sprang up and the boys followed. While the clock ticked away the seconds and McKing stared and the Bedford fans booed and the Burnside fans held their breath, Rich, Greg, and Danny bandied the ball around. Finally the gun went off. 51-49, Burnside over Bedford.

Down in the locker room the Bats were weary but jubilant. "Well, we took that one," Danny said breathlessly. "I wasn't sure we would for a while, but we did."

"That was a good workout."

"We whipped those black boys! YA-HOO!" Rich shrieked. "I wouldn't have lost that game for nothing. Did you guys dig the way they pick names of bugs for themselves? 'Beetles,' 'Roach'—that's really the hot one."

"Don't forget 'Daddy Longlegs.'"

"They oughta' call themselves the Bedford Bedbugs," said one of the sophomores.

"Pretty good, Knox. Pretty good."

"Funny, funny," Greg muttered to himself at the corner of the locker room where he dressed by himself. Skinny yellow punks, he thought. He almost hated them now. Get in good with Rich. With the big boy. The tough guy. Right now he wished he were home sprawled out on the couch, watching TV and sipping a cool vanilla shake. He sighed. But he was fifty-five miles from home, and there was a bad scene coming up with Virginia.

He went to the mirror to comb his hair, and for a minute,

the laughter, the talk, the rush of water behind him, all dissolved into one din that belonged to another world. Then he tensed with anger. But if any of those jerks said something to him, he'd come up with something that would shock their drawers off.

Overtures came soon enough. "Hey, Greg?" Danny hollered over.

"Yeah?"

"Do you have room for two more in your car?"

"To go home?"

"And for the cruise. Hank's car broke down and he and Barbara had to come by chartered bus. Naturally they want to stay around for the cruising."

"What do you mean?" Although Greg knew darned well what Danny meant. The gang had been talking about it all week, about how they were going to joy ride around Bedford for kicks after the game—"touring," as Jake would say. A year ago he himself might have done it, but now the idea seemed callous.

He was surprised that any of them would think he'd want to go, but it was Virginia's thoughtlessness that bothered him most. All week she had chattered about it, who was taking cars, who was riding with whom, what everybody was wearing, what time they expected to be home, what they were telling their parents—about everything except whether or not he wanted to go. At first he was baffled, then disappointed and hurt, then angry. He had waited and waited for her to ask him how he felt about it, but she didn't, and time ran out. Now he would fix her. He would show her that he wasn't her shadow, he wouldn't follow her without thought or will, wherever she went. But he would play dumb, as he was doing with Danny.

"Well, Greg?" Danny said impatiently. "The cruise. The cruise. Do you have room for two or not? I have to run out and tell them."

"As far as I'm concerned," Greg said casually, "there's room for three. It's Virginia's car tonight, and I'm not going."

95

Danny gawked at Greg. Some of the other boys knew what was going on. They glanced at each other knowingly waiting for the rest.

Rich laughed out loud. "He doesn't have to go cruising to see how the darker half lives. He loafs with them."

"Why don't you shut your trap, Wallace?" Greg said coolly. "Haven't you mouthed off enough for one night? It's a wonder you don't get trench mouth from all the filth that comes out of it."

Rich swore. The boys were bug-eyed. Davis wasn't taking anything these days. Rich narrowed his eyes. "Do you want to keep playing ball for Burnside?"

"You know, I really don't care."

Rich cupped his hand by his ear as though he hadn't heard. "What was that, Davis?"

"I said, I don't really care."

Rich looked around at the other boys. "There's a good man to play ball with."

"Uh . . . you know, Greg," Frank broke in, "Virginia's gonna be pretty surprised."

"That might do her good."

"It's her car, anyway," said Rich. "I think we can dig up a date for her. A lot of guys would like to take her out."

"Can't blame them for that," Greg said as he opened the door to leave. "She's sharp."

He walked upstairs and headed for the main hall of the high school. He had to get to the gang before the boys did. A night watchman was sitting on a chair with his arms crossed by the main door.

"Hey, man," the old Negro in the overalls and railroad cap drawled, "you a basketball player?"

"Yes."

"You ain't supposed to be walking around the school heah. You suppose to go out the back exit downstairs. My man Higgins is down there countin' heads."

"Oh . . . that's right. Sorry, I forgot. I'll go back."

"Wall, since you all the way up heah, might as well go out the front. I'll just hurry on down and tell Higgins one is already gone." He rose and went with Greg to the door.

"Thanks. Thanks a lot." Well, that turned out to be a break, thought Greg. It would save him the time of walking around from the back of the building. As he went down the main steps of the dingy building, he saw a large crowd of Burnside rooters waiting out in front. The chartered buses were parked along the street.

Now for the showdown with Virginia. She would be out in front somewhere with Tony and Mona and some of the other juniors. Like a man sobering up and regretting things he had done, Greg began to feel a little ashamed of the game he was playing with Virginia. To justify it now, he tried to recall the anger he had felt those times when she had so thoughtlessly included him in the gang's plans. She knew what had happened on Monday at practice. Hadn't it occurred to her that to go on this disgusting ride would look like he was selling himself out? She had been acting awfully funny lately. As he neared the crowd in which Virginia was somewhere waiting, the bitter memories began to soften his feeling of guilt and regret. He even managed to feel a little angry again.

He was near the gate and he strained his eyes to find her. Nobody familiar. Most of the characters milling around the fence were freshmen and sophomores who stared in awe and vague recognition as he came through the gate. "Greg Davis. . . . Greg Davis. . . ." He heard them mutter as he sidled through the crowd. He still didn't see anyone he knew. It was just like the gang to stand off cool-like somewhere so they wouldn't look like they belonged to the rest of the mob. Accursed game of hide-and-seek, he thought. It was like having to find someone so they could give you a slap in the face. He was tired and the game was over. He wondered how it happened that he was on this strange, dark street in Slumsville playing Find-the-Cool-Cats with some very un-cool people, instead of heading for home.

At last he spotted them standing in front of a drugstore way over on the next block. He cursed. To have to walk all the way over to those jerks. He became conscious of—not a loneliness—but of a singularity. Right now, he realized with dizziness, there was no one like him. He had always fitted into some group, but right now, he wasn't part of anything or anyone—not of the group he approached, nor of the boys on the team, nor of the younger students boarding the buses. He walked more quickly now, having mustered strength and confidence from his own uniqueness.

And there they were—the enemy. He was nearing the street corner now and smiled ironically at his sudden sense of drama. They were all trying to look properly blasé and sophisticated; to him they looked so small, so helpless, so utterly the same with their self-conscious savoir-faire. Virginia was smashingly dressed, as usual, wearing a sweater that would have cost him at least two weeks salary at the park. And she was trying to smoke. How ridiculous she looked to him, gasping and puffing and trying to chatter through the tattletale novice's cloud she had blown around herself. He wanted to laugh in her face; but he was feeling too somber. He wanted her to get sick and have to excuse herself to barf around the corner, and everyone would know why. That would fix her. What was the matter with Virginia, anyway? She wasn't a stupid girl and she had talent. What made a girl like that act like such a sheep and be so insensitive.

All too soon Greg's private harlequinade was over. Tony Stafford spotted him, and he was transformed from spectator to player. He straightened to go into his act. "Let's have one for Davis!" Tony called, and the small group applauded and cheered. Hmph. Nice of them, Greg grudgingly admitted, and for a moment he felt like a heel. But then he realized that they weren't cheering for him anyway. They were cheering for themselves, because he was somebody and he was part of their crowd.

He smiled stiffly and greeted the group. Virginia stepped

forward and took him by the arm. "Where's everybody else?" she said.

"They're poking around. Chewing the fat. I hurried."

"Why didn't you wait for them?"

"Can't a guy walk by himself?" Greg asked softly. They'd be along soon, he thought, and they knew what he was up to. So he had to make things clear right away. He swallowed and flexed his hands. Then he said loudly but carefully, "I wish they'd hurry. It's a long way home. And you can't tell what might happen around here."

No response. Some of the kids hadn't even been listening.

He looked at his watch ostentatiously and said, "Nine-thirty-five. We'll be lucky if we make it home by eleven."

It worked on Virginia. "What are you talking about? We'll be here until eleven."

"Where?"

"Here. In Bedford, silly."

"What for?"

"The cruise. Remember?"

"Nobody said anything to me about it."

"Then you must have been in a trance. You heard me talking about it all week."

"Yes. I did. That's not what I said. I said, nobody said anything to me about it."

Virginia rolled her eyes. "What's the matter with you, Greg? Do you need an engraved invitation?"

"No, but I would have liked the chance to refuse."

"Huh?" Virginia was too confused to understand, but the others did. They looked at each other slyly, knowingly. "Check him!" someone murmured. Then they stared.

Greg flinched a little when he noticed their expressions, but he quickly insisted to himself that he was right. Tony Stafford put his hand on Virginia's shoulder as if to protect her from a cad. Well, maybe he was being a cad for making a fool out of her in front of everyone; she wasn't the only one to blame. He was getting sick of the farce anyway.

99

He spoke out boldly. "All right, Virginia . . . everybody . . . let's play it straight. You know without anybody telling you, that what you're doing is . . . is stupid and childish. . . ."

"A sermon from Reverend Davis!"

"It's a rotten way to have fun. I thought maybe you'd realize by now that I wouldn't want to have anything to do with treating a whole group of people like freaks, but you don't realize anything. If you can't figure it out for yourself, I'll tell you now. The whole idea makes me sick. If you want to leer at a dirty, crummy town with a lot of poor people in it, go ahead. But count me out. Sorry, Virginia. You'll have to get someone else."

"Greg, it doesn't have anything to do with Jake. It won't hurt him. We aren't going to hurt anybody."

"That doesn't change the fact that it's rotten and crummy."

Greg was ready to leave. No one had anything to say. But he waited for a response from Virginia. She just looked at him—a little confused, a little surprised, a little . . . something else now. He was sorry he had sacrificed Virginia's dignity to the pack of wolves just to spite them. He could see they were enjoying her humiliation. Spite? he thought a second time. Nothing more than that? he thought sadly. He wasn't sure.

After an awkward silence Tony Stafford spoke up. With an effeminate wave of the hand, he said, "We can get you a date, honey. Don't worry. Anyone know if Rich is dated up for tonight?"

The big fruit, thought Greg.

"Yeah. That new girl, Vicki."

"Well, you can be my date for tonight, Ginny," Tony said, patting her shoulder.

The kids smiled at each other again. Ghouls, thought Greg.

Virginia stepped up to Greg. "How will you get home, Greg? I promised these kids. . . ."

"It's all right, baby. I can squeeze in one of the buses."

"You sure you don't want. . . ."

"N-no. I'd better go. I'll call you tomorrow."

"Tomorrow's the party, Greg. I've already made the costumes."

"I know, honey. Don't worry. We'll go. I promise." He squeezed her hand gently and quickly walked away.

Ah yes, the party, Greg thought as he walked back to the buses. Three times Virginia had fitted him for his costume. Once she took his measurements; the second time she wanted to fit a lining; the third time she had added some kind of padding and wanted to check it for shape. It was something elaborate, no doubt about that. On Wednesday she had brought to school, of all things, blue rubber swim fins to check size. He couldn't figure that one out.

He liked the headpiece which covered the whole head and had slits for the eyes, nose and mouth. He would feel private, safe and anonymous under a mask like that. He might even be able to grumble and make faces at people under it, he thought wryly. He sighed. What sense was there in getting so filled up with hatred? It only made you feel sick. People would probably be in a party mood and forget things —he hoped.

There were still three chartered buses by Bedford High School. He looked for someone he knew and spotted Mary Hines, a ninth grade member of the Junior History Club. She was a little girl, all right, but she was still female. And he'd charm her. "Hello, Mary," Greg said warmly. She turned and looked up, surprised. "Are you on one of the buses?" he asked.

"Yes," she answered.

"Do you know if there's any extra room?"

"Golly, no. Some of the students were standing on the way. You have to have a ticket anyway."

"Hmm." Greg bent over and said softly, "Would you vouch for me if I said I was a Burnside student and was stranded? I'll offer the driver half fare."

"Well . . . sure. I . . . guess that would be all right."

"You're nice and light, you could sit on my lap."

Mary reddened, stared and gulped. "Well . . . we'd better talk to the driver now. There he is."

The bus was filled the junior high school students who sang the high school songs and got pretty silly after a while. But they had a good time in a goofy sort of way. Greg did too.

———✦———

"Blue ducks!" Greg hollered. "Hey, this is pretty crazy."

"Well, I'm glad you're pleased," said Virginia.

The costumes, complete with wings, covered just about every inch of them from head to toe. Virginia had sewn leaf-shaped, blue oilcloth "feathers" over the entire lining and had made large pink papier-mâché bills. She told Greg to dig up a blue shirt or jersey; something light and cool but with long sleeves; and now she strapped the cardboard wings above his elbows so that they covered his outer arms but still left his hands free. The bell-shaped costumes came just above their knees, and below that they both wore pink knee-socks. On their feet were the blue swim fins.

"They're not too hard to walk in," Virginia laughed, "if you lift up your whole foot like this."

"And it's awfully good exercise for the thighs," Greg said in an old woman's voice.

"We can take them off when we dance."

Virginia's parents had taken the car but the huge Wallace house was only five blocks from Virginia's and they were walking to the party. They couldn't really sit anyway, and it gave them a chance to show off.

"What time did you get home last night?" Greg asked along the way.

"Around eleven-thirty."

"Eleven-thirty?" said Greg, perplexed. He himself had gotten home at eleven by bus. "Kind of early, considering, wasn't it?"

"All right. I didn't bring it up, so don't start."

"Huh? All I said was, what time did you get home? I wasn't lecturing. Didn't you hear me?"

"I heard you. It didn't take long."

"Seems like it took no time. You must've had a five minute cruise."

"Why do you have to keep it up?" Virginia cried. "Why start a fight over it?"

"What's the matter with you? I ask you something in a nice way and you get mad."

"If you're trying to act dumb you're not being very subtle. But it sounds to me like you're just trying to rub it in. Why, Greg? Why needle me before a party?"

"What? It sounds like we're talking about two different things. I asked you in a nice way how long you went riding around Bedford last night. I was just curious, that's all. What are you snapping about?"

"Do you . . . do you mean you don't know what happened?"

Greg looked at her. "I knew you were taking a cruise, that's all."

"Well, there was no cruise after . . . after. . . ."

"After what? What happened?"

"The boys were jumped. Didn't you know about it?"

"No kidding! Who got jumped? Where?"

"The team. Some colored kids, the Bedford players and a few others, were waiting for them when they came out of the locker rooms last night. You met us early. I guess they weren't there when you came out. You were lucky. By yourself like that, they would have creamed you."

"I came out a different door. I was in a hurry to get to you; I was pretty mad about that cruise business and I wandered out the front door. Anyway, what happened? Did anybody get hurt?"

"Frankie. All the boys got cuts and bruises, they were treated at the Bedford County Hospital, but Frankie got it the worst."

They stopped on the sidewalk. Greg's heart swelled and his throat became full and thick. Frankie. Frankie was the gentle one. He probably didn't even know how to fight.

"He had to stay overnight and the last I heard of it, his mother and dad came and got him this afternoon."

"He's . . . he's all right, then?"

"I guess so."

Greg grieved at the unfairness of it. Sometimes the mean guys started it all and got off without a scratch. Made you wish somebody was up there pulling the strings. Rich should spit his hatred and sickness . . . yes, there had to be something wrong with that guy's head, something that messed him up when he was a kid . . . and a guy like Frankie, who wouldn't hurt a fly, should feel the fists and shed the blood . . . where was the justice?

"Did they have knives?"

"No. I don't think so. I guess they were frisked before they went into the school."

"They probably didn't know it was going to happen themselves."

"What? Oh, come on. You mean they didn't know until they lost the game."

"I don't think they worry about things like winning basketball games.

"Well, I hope you're convinced, Greg. Now you see what they're like."

"Virginia . . . I'm not saying that what they did was right, but let me tell you, what Rich did on the basketball court last night was enough to get him his teeth knocked out all over the floor."

"Don't blame it on him, Greg."

Greg curled his fists in frustration. The way Rich managed to work things, you really couldn't put the blame right on him. He was a real pro at starting trouble. "Let's not argue about it," he said. "Tell me the rest. How many guys were involved? How long did it last? Who broke it up?"

"Carl said he saw their first team plus a couple of guys from the bench. Rich says it was their whole team against our whole team."

"Hmph. Sounds like a kind of impromptu thing made up in the locker room."

"It didn't last too long. Apparently, they had policemen around to look out for something like that, but the guys got their lumps anyway."

"It's a good thing everybody will be wearing masks tonight. Anyway, maybe it's good that it stopped where it did, behind the school, or you might have battle scars to hide, too. Poor Frankie. Is he coming to the party?"

"Louise says yes."

Greg sighed. "That's amazing. I don't know how I went the whole day without hearing about it from anybody. Of course, I was working. . . ."

"Well, to put it bluntly, Greg, you've put yourself out of the mainstream of things. You work and you seem to have cut yourself off from the gang; you even walked out on the team yesterday."

"I wish you wouldn't put it that way, Virginia. I left the locker room early yesterday so I could tell you I was going straight home without an audience."

"The news broke to the parents right at Frank's home. They were practically all there for a Civic League meeting. And since your parents aren't members, they didn't hear. You must have been home by that time anyway. And I guess people think you and . . . and your family aren't interested in what goes on in Burnside."

"You mean because they're not members of that . . . Micky Mouse Club? My father says he wouldn't waste his time. He says all they do is gossip and pat each other on the back. He says. . . ."

"Well, they're doing something about last night!" Virginia said hotly.

"What?"

"They're calling for the suspension of the Bedford team from the Interstate Athletic Association, maybe from more, and for the expulsion of the players from school."

"Jeez! Is that what the Citizen's Deportment Council does?"

"So . . . if I were you, Greg, I wouldn't bring that . . . that Negro around here for a while, because everyone's really down on them now."

"Jake! He was seventy miles away. He doesn't have anything to do with it! And what are they going to do about Rich Wallace's 'department'?"

"Why do you always blame Rich? All right. So Rich has a big mouth. Didn't you ever sing that song when you were a child, 'Sticks and stones may break my bones, but names can never harm me'? Well, I'd rather take my chances with Rich than with a a pack of Negroes who go around attacking people. Now . . . can we go on? We must have been standing here for fifteen minutes."

"Do you expect me to go to that party now? At Rich's house? How can I go to that party?"

The girl's face was a mixture of sadness and anger.

"I know. I know. You spent weeks on these costumes. Jeez! I . . . I don't know what to do." He swore. "Here. I'll just pull this headpiece down and hide under it all night. There. Now I don't care what goes on."

Soon they were laboriously climbing up the steps to the door of the Wallace home. "Ooooo," Virginia squealed when they reached the porch. "I'll bet the kids will drop everything when they see us. I'll bet everybody will be dressed practically the same—in trite old things as hoboes and flappers. We'll really stand out." It was as though no strong words had just passed between them. "Mona's giving a prize, you know, for best costumes. Wait—don't ring the bell yet." She fluffed a few crucial feathers on both costumes and straightened Greg's enormous polka-dot tie.

"These are some costumes, Virginia. It must have taken days to make them."

106

"Not really, when you know how to do it. And since my steady is so unavailable these days. . . ."

"But your school work, doll. You said you were going to crack down on the studies since I've been so busy."

"Now, stop lecturing, professor. You're too serious for your age, Greg. Besides"—she stepped back, still examining Greg's costume—"I study enough. For a dancer, anyway. Now we're going to a big party. Mona said a hundred kids might be here." She pressed the doorbell.

In a few moments the door was opening—very, very slowly. Someone was behind it, simulating a squeaking door. Greg and Virginia waited tensely—shifting, giggling—then there was a shrill scream. The door flew open wide and out jumped a vampire. "Too much. Too much, Mona," Virginia giggled.

Mona wore a long black taffeta gown, white make-up, something blue on her lips and a long, black wig. In one scarlet, false-fingered hand she held a foot-long cigarette holder; in the other, a red-tinted beverage. Her childish squeals on seeing the ducks were anything but diabolic. "Who's this?" she squeaked delighted. A pleased giggle came from Virginia; under his mask, Greg smiled.

"Even if we don't know you, come in. You deserve it," said Mona, stepping back to hold the door.

"Ginny and Greg," Virginia whispered as they passed. "Don't tell anyone."

"Look at this!" Mona hollered. "Look at this, everybody!" Above the din her voice reached only a few of the guests, but the costumes drew their own attention.

Rich was standing by the fireplace, surrounded by members of the basketball team, regular sidekicks like Henry and Skippy, assorted sophomore and junior admirers, and his latest girl, Vicki. Virginia drifted over to her host, and Greg reluctantly followed, wishing that he could black out for the next few minutes and parade his costume in some mindless, robot-like state. Above the admiring "Ooooo's" of the fireplace cabal, Rich hollered, "Who is it?"

Virginia let out the secret and excitedly waited for compliments.

"SOUL brother!" Rich hollered. Everyone grew silent. "Everybody know what 'soul brother' is? It's from the riots. The yellow niggers wrote 'soul brother' on their windows, and they didn't get messed up. Now Davis here, he didn't get messed up last night. Do you suppose he was wearing a sign 'Soul Brother' when he came out that back door last night?"

Greg was speechless. Under his mask he muttered, "Good God!" and slowly shook his head. Rich Wallace was cracking up with hate.

"See the chicken-bird shake his head? Davis, I thought you were gonna come as Abe Lincoln or something."

It was time for Greg to speak out, stupefied as he was. He waited for a few moments until everyone was quiet, then he said, "I thought you'd come as Adolf Hitler." The remark was more serious than cutting or clever, but Greg was satisfied with the murmuring it drew. Then he slowly walked up to Rich Wallace and slipped off his mask, he fingered Rich's opulent eighteenth-century costume; then spoke again. "It looks like you came as a fruit. That's in pretty good character, anyway. And if it gets too hot for you in here, Rich, you can slip off all these flitty rags and walk around as a jackass." No sounds. "But keep your mask on. You don't want anybody to know you finally got yours."

"It takes Davis a long time."

"Stop it, both of you!" Virginia squeezed in between them and pushed Greg hard in the chest, back and away out of the crowd. "Why, why, WHY, Greg? Why does it always have to be like this? It isn't even funny anymore."

"Funny? When was it ever funny?"

"Rich was always loud. And everybody laughed and forgot about it."

"That's why he is the way he is."

"So why is it so serious between you two now?"

"You know why."

"Because he hates Negroes?"

"Because he hates everybody. He's some kind of a nut, but you idiots are too dumb to see it. You think he's a funny boy, and he bullies you and he gets away with it."

"Oh, you're exaggerating. Don't be so dramatic."

"Ever watch him chewing a pencil in class? He looks like he's gonna crack up right on the spot."

"So maybe he's a little nervous. Mona told me he was sick when he was a kid."

"It must have affected his brain."

"And his father used to pick on him because he wasn't . . . oh, athletic and stuff. So he's had his troubles."

"That doesn't give him an excuse to pick on the rest of the world."

"Rich is entitled to his opinion."

"I wouldn't call pushing people around and calling them dirty names expressing an opinion."

"I never heard him mention anybody by name."

"Of course not. Wallace is too sneaky for that. He knows just where to draw the line so he doesn't get busted in the teeth."

Virginia sighed. "I don't know what to say to you, Greg. You're entitled to pick your own friends, but if you keep putting on a show, you're just asking for trouble."

"Keep out of the way of the bully, huh?"

"You'd better keep that colored boy out of the way."

"Don't worry. Jake can take care of himself."

"I'm sure he can."

"Don't you get smart."

"You can be his friend around his own digs. You don't have to ask for it by bringing him here."

"My friends can come wherever I ask them. Jake's coming to see me tomorrow."

"You're just being stubborn."

"I'm not going to carry a typewriter around town because I'm scared of Rich Wallace; Jake's coming over."

109

"Suit yourself. Look . . . let's make peace, all right. Let's not spoil the party over it."

"As far as I'm concerned it's already spoiled."

"Greg! Oh, Greg!" And with a wave of her feathered hand Virginia tried to shoo the whole incident away.

"Don't rain on your parade," Greg muttered softly. Even she was selling him out.

Greg felt especially played out Monday after school. Maybe his full schedule was getting the best of him, he thought, as he untied his gym shoes. He had stayed up so late yesterday. There had been the game, work, the party; and Jake had come over to have some of his notes typed. It left him homework to do well into the night. He blinked his eyes.

The black gym doors swung open. Rich Wallace stomped into the locker room, his wet hair clawing his brow, his gray eyes narrowed and sparkling as he glared into Greg's own. "Hey, Davis!"

Greg looked up.

"Skip told me you had that colored guy around here again."

"So what?" Jake had mentioned seeing "that boy who works at the drugstore" on the crosstown bus. Greg felt sad. Across his mind ran an ugly picture of Skip telling the news to Rich, feeding his hatred. Jake had been so chipper lately he had probably even said hello. It was sickening. Greg chilled at the irony, forgetting that Rich was there.

But Rich Wallace wasn't interested in replies. Before Greg even looked up at him, Rich put his foot on the bench, bent down and spoke right into Greg's face. "I don't care who you want to loaf with but keep them where they belong. We don't want 'em around here."

They had exchanged many words these past couple of weeks, but this time Greg felt assaulted. Rich's warm breath

110

on his face could have been a poke with a stick; he jerked away and looked up. Now some of the other boys had come in. Greg shouted. "You may be the captain of this ball team, Wallace, but you're not dictator of the world, you hear? I'll pick my own friends and I'll take them where I want, so you'd better get that through your thick skull. Now get off my back and don't ever say a word to me again."

"Look Davis. You'd better pick your side."

"What do you mean by that?"

"I mean you're either with us or against us. And it didn't look like you were with us at the game Friday."

"Because I wouldn't huck those guys like you did, sport?"

"Because you were too busy nigger lovin' . . . ."

Greg stopped thinking. His fingers clenched automatically as he took in the sure maliciousness in Rich's cold eyes; his body stiffened as he faced the tough chin, the tough face. He barely knew it was happening. It was just . . . smash! His fist landed on Rich's square chin, and Rich stumbled backwards. He hadn't hit him too hard—in that last split second before contact Greg had subconsciously checked his power. Now he felt ashamed and confused. He almost wanted to apologize. But Rich lunged at him. And in his shock he wasn't ready. He fell down, shook his head, and when he looked up, knew there would be more. Rich was waiting for him with clenched fists. He caught a glimpse of the boys and felt sick. They looked like strangers now, standing immobile with diabolic interest. Greg had to protect himself. He came back desperately strong, punching Rich in the shoulders and chest, hoping to pin him back somewhere and stop. The lockers rattled as Rich's back slammed on them. But Rich was strong and Rich was mad; he came back and beat Greg on the head—on the left, on the right, on the left. . . . Greg gasped with each thud, lifted his hands to check the blows and things began to get dark. . . .

"What the hell!" Coach McKing's shriek startled everyone. Greg and Rich halted, heaving hoarsely, while the other boys winced at McKing's outraged cursing. McKing's face was bright red and his eyes sparkled like two hot coals. He was screaming in a woman's voice: "What the hell's going on here? What's this all about?" He looked around at the timid spectators and spit on the floor. "Buncha. . . . Not a word gets outta this locker room, d'ya hear me? Now, get-outta-here," he said threateningly.

He quieted down while the boys left the scene. Greg and Rich waited. The only sound was the rasp of their breathing. McKing glanced around, then asked, with a surprising lack of sharpness, "What's the matter, boys?"

"I don't know about Davis," said Rich, "but I don't feel like talking now."

"Me neither," said Greg.

"You boys get dressed and go home. I'll talk to you later."

On the way home, Greg felt sick and very confused. He wondered how it all had happened. He hadn't been in a fight since he was a kid about nine years old. How could such a dirty, lousy thing have happened to him now? A fight in school? That was strictly for punks. He grimaced and sucked in his breath. It hurt. He hoped there wasn't anything on his face for Mom and Dad to see. He hadn't even looked in the mirror before he left.

DETACHMENT

It was Wednesday and home-room period. Greg was glad it was almost time to go home. By now the kids had heard about the fight and they had been looking at him queerly all day. He didn't feel like doing homework. He'd try to think about a topic for his Problems of Democracy paper. Most of the kids had already had their selections approved, but he still hadn't even the faintest idea of what to write about.

He turned. A freshman had just come into the room and handed a note to Miss Wright. She called to the back of the room. "Gregory!"

"Yes, Miss Wright?"

"Mr. McKing would like to see you."

Ugh, thought Greg. "All right," he said. His stomach got fluttery. He went down to the basement to the coach's office. Frankie Klinglehaus was just leaving. He said hello to Greg and breezed by.

McKing's arm was propped up on the table and he hid his face behind a clenched fist. He looked troubled and his tenseness was contagious. Greg braced himself for something unpleasant. "You wanted to see me, Coach?" he said.

McKing sighed. "Yeah, Greg. I did." He couldn't seem to

get started. Finally he said, "I guess you know what's on my mind."

Greg swallowed. "Yes, sir. I think I do."

Then McKing plunged right in. "You just can't have a ball team when the guys are breaking out in fist fights."

"I know," Greg said sadly.

"I don't really know what's between you and Wallace, but I do want to know what you intend to do about it."

"Didn't Frank tell you?"

McKing reddened. He was upset, all right.

"I'm sorry. I shouldn't have said that," said Greg.

"I don't make it a policy to rely on gossip when I want to know something," said McKing. "If I wanted to know what you and Wallace were fighting about—and I don't, incidentally—I'd ask you and Wallace. Not Frank, not Danny, not Carl—nobody. Just you and Wallace. Now Frankie was here on an entirely different matter." McKing glanced into Greg's eyes, then looked down quickly, focussing interest on bits of paper he was pushing around with an eraser tip.

He doesn't want to know? thought Greg. Then what was there to talk about? Greg felt dumb just sitting there and overcome with that lonely feeling he had been having lately. McKing didn't want to know. What was right and what was wrong didn't matter. He just didn't want two little boys messing up his gym and his team. He just didn't want someone to make his job tougher for him. What was there to say?

McKing seeing Greg's bewilderment went on. "All I want to know is, are you going to settle things between you soon? Because if you don't, it's going to show real bad. The season'll be starting." Greg remained silent. "Now this wasn't one little isolated fight. Something has been going on for weeks now and it looks bad. It doesn't look like a small thing."

Greg turned over McKing's inplications in his mind. But he wasn't going to give in to Rich and sweep things under

114

the rug for McKing. "You're right," he said. "It isn't a small thing. Rich has got to lay off, and that's only part of it."

Knowing McKing, Greg expected him to sound off with some ready-made compromise like, stop blaming Rich—it takes two to make a fight. But to his surprise, McKing looked baffled. Finally he spoke. "Greg, look . . . I can't arbitrate here. Whatever I think. . . . it's not my job to hang what I think on somebody else, y'understand? Now . . . I do know a little. I'll . . . I'll be honest. I know what it's about. But I don't know all the facts, see?" Greg nodded. "It's not my job to tell anybody else what they should think in their private lives, and even if it was, I couldn't do it." The coach looked up, a pleading, silly smile on his face. "I mean, not that I wouldn't want to. But I couldn't brainwash somebody in ten seconds. Or even ten hours or days or. . . . Do you see what I mean?"

"Yes, sir."

"And Greg . . . I don't think you could, either. Even if you're sure you're right. You're just up against too much. Bigger people than you. . . ."

"I know all that, sir," said Greg. He felt fed up with Mc-King's stammering and apologizing and preaching of the obvious. "I wasn't trying to change anyone, Coach. But I don't want anybody to try to tell me what to do either. I just want to be left alone."

"Yeah. Well, it's a problem, I know. Wallace is . . . a little funny. You just have to get used to him, that's all, just like everybody else in this world. Everybody's a little funny in some way. That's where teamwork comes in. A bunch of guys give in and pull together. You're a smart boy, Greg. You could probably work it out better'n I ever could. The fact remains, I have a ball team to run. And two guys can't play together when they're fighting."

"I know. I've been thinking about it. And I guess the only answer is . . . for me to quit." Greg lowered his head, barely letting the words escape.

"I don't like to hear that, Greg," McKing said.

"I don't like to say it, Coach. And I didn't know I was going to say it when I walked in here."

"Greg, don't say anything you don't mean."

"Coach, I'm not just saying it. I don't want to quit the team, but I just don't see any other way."

"What about . . . things like . . . teamwork and sportsmanship?"

Greg controlled the urge to moan out loud. "Coach," he began slowly, "I think there's more to it than just giving in a little here and pulling together there. Sometimes things are just plain right and wrong and you've gotta pick your side."

"Look . . . I know you've been taught about all men are created equal and about standing up for what's right. But in real life, it just doesn't always work out so neat. Sometimes the poor sap who stands up and does something gets left holding the bag, know what I mean? You think everybody else is gonna follow you like Joan of Arc, but when the chips are down they all ride the other way. Maybe the best thing to do is just mind your own business and make it as good as you can for yourself without stepping on somebody else's toes. Now I know it ain't that way in books and in church, but in real life. . . ."

"Well . . . right now I don't know what I'd do if it came to hurting my skin, but in this case it's not going to cost me much to . . . stand up, like you say."

"Isn't it? What about the prestige you have around here?"

Greg shrugged his shoulders. "I'll be out of this place in a year and a half."

"What about scholarships?"

"Well, I guess I'm pretty lucky, Coach. My grades are good, a couple of important teachers like me, and I have a couple of other things going for me. Maybe that's why I'm in a position to do this. Maybe if I didn't have all these things going for me, I wouldn't be so . . . self-righteous. I don't know." Greg shook his head. "I don't know what to think. I used to think that being . . . that having moral courage was a matter of free will and conscience. Now I wonder if even that isn't a matter of breaks—of being born with or without the angels on your side."

"Ha!" McKing shook his head and laughed. "You're getting too deep for me."

"Anyway, as long as things are on my side and as long as I have a little guts and . . . character, I might just as well use it before it gets moldy."

"Yeah. I guess I oughta be ashamed, an old buck like me telling a kid like you to sell out. But there's something else."

"What's that?"

"Don't you feel that if you quit, Rich beat you?"

"No, sir. I don't. You said yourself that you couldn't change somebody even if you really wanted to. I certainly can't change Wallace. I think there's something terribly wrong with him. He's sick, Coach. He needs a headshrinker. I wouldn't do him any good by sticking around. It's just the opposite. I might be doing him harm by giving him more opportunities to . . . to. . . . Do you know what I mean?"

"I think so," McKing said slowly. He stared into space, deep in thought. Suddenly the bell sounded—an old-fashioned one that whirred and rattled around their ears. McKing and Greg, startled, looked up angrily at the tarnished cup, high and inaccessible, above the doorway. But they remained sitting, somber and silent. Greg studied McKing's face. He had been a good coach. And he understood more than he admitted once you wore down his rough surface.

Finally Greg spoke. "You know, I almost hate to make a move."

"Oh, yeah?"

"Uh-huh. Makes it kind of final, I guess, to walk out of here."

"To tell you the truth, I'm sorry it's you who's walking out."

117

Greg smiled. "Thanks, Coach. Even though I know I'm right, I feel dirty."

"Why?"

"Well, when you drop off a school team like this, it's usually because something's wrong."

"Something is wrong."

"I mean cheating or flunking or something. You just don't do it."

"Maybe that's the trouble, Greg. Most people don't have the guts or brains to pull away from something that's wrong. They just stick around like a bunch of yellow bellies and the wrong person gets the dirty end of it. Look, boy; anybody asks me anything, you're clean. Now let's get out of here." McKing plunked his hat on his head. "Greg?"

"Yes, sir?"

McKing held out his hand. "I enjoyed working with you."

"Thanks, Coach," said Greg as he shook the red hand.

"Greg?"

"Yes?"

"If you change your mind, drop around and see me."

Greg nodded.

Everybody was in the hall now. He could hear them as he forced himself up the stairs. He wished he could linger on the stairway until they were all gone. He felt they would read on his face what he had just done, but he had to get his books out of home room before Miss Wright locked the door.

———

Greg took his lunch tray to the back ot the cafeteria and sat in an extreme corner of the room. Thank goodness this wretched week was over, he thought, mindful that it was Friday. On Wednesday, after he came home from school, he felt he had to tell somebody about the break he had made, and after supper he told his family the whole story. "You won't be sorry," his father had said, and that made him feel better.

But in school he had been in an uncomfortable spot. He wasn't about to go around making a formal announcement of his leaving the team; he couldn't have put up with the goggle eyes, the gaping mouths, the phony innocence, the sham sympathy, the malicious request for details. Then, too, there was always the chance that the story had gotten out anyway, and someone might have said, "So what?" and made him feel like a dope who overestimated his own importance. So he had to walk around all day wondering who knew and what they thought.

But after school things had officially popped. He hadn't been at practice, and McKing told the boys that Greg was no longer with them. Everyone else had gotten the news via the phones. Virginia knew and called him up immediately. She had been told by Mona, and when Mona knew something, it was like having it in the newspaper. Greg was inclined to think that the whole thing had something to do with Virginia's excusing herself to eat lunch with the girls today.

With it all out in the open, though, he felt relieved, if not irritated with Burnside Heights High School and everyone in it. All of them looked so caught up in the Burnside whirl that they seemed not to have a minute for thoughts of their own. He knew the feeling, for he had gone through it himself—the collective judgments, the collective actions. At one table a lively group of freshman girls, most of them tiny and thin, looked like ludicrous doll versions of the junior and senior girls whose styles of dress and hair they copied. Dolls you saw in the stores nowadays were just like that, Greg thought—stylish clothes draping small, stick-like bodies, sophisticated hair-dos framing wide-eyed baby faces.

At another table, a lanky sophomore Greg knew from History Club was just sitting down with his girlfriend, looking self-conscious and awkward as he unloaded her tray and listened to every word she was saying. For things like this

Greg felt a warm nostalgia; as for most of it, though, he was glad it was over. It was like an ailment, that anxiety over whether you were doing just the right thing and doing it just right; whether you looked right, whether you said the right thing, whether you would get that letter or sorority pin or medal or whatever you were after.

Everyone wanted to be "with it," even the clumsy freshman boys at Greg's table who thought they were rejecting the standards of their more debonair peers. Whether or not they realized it, they slurped their soup, exchanged insults, made funny noises and otherwise rejected the social amenities with a kind of fraternity.

He was in the perfect mood, calm, mildly amused, but then he saw Carl, Danny, Frank and Henry wandering back slowly and looking for him. Who else would be in that forsaken corner of the cafeteria? Finally Danny saw him and nodded. He turned to the other boys and they started to come over. When they finally reached him they shifted around nervously, and for a few moments there were no words except mumbled hello's.

Greg, feeling giddy and smug and knowing why they were there, took advantage of their uneasiness. "Where's the chief?" he said. "I want to see the chief himself."

"Aw, come off it, Greg," said Danny. "Rich is busy. He knew we were gonna talk to you. He wanted us to. But he couldn't make it now."

Greg nodded with mock understanding. "Sure. Sure. I know. The chief is a busy man. A big man. He gotta lotta organizin' to do," he said gangster-fashion.

"Don't carry a chip on your shoulder, Greg," said Carl.

"Who? Me? Oooo. . . . Jeez," said Greg, frantically brushing his shoulder. "Never let it be said that Davis is lookin' for a fight, especially wit' da organization."

"Don't do us any favors, Greg."

"Aw, don't give us a rough time, Greg."

"We feel bad enough, Greg," said Danny. "A fight . . . that's pretty serious."

"Yeah. Sure it is. But we could have punched ourselves right out of Burnside High School and you guys would have stood there waiting for blood."

"What could we have done, Greg?" said Frank. "We were so surprised. We didn't know what to do. Did you expect us to break it up?"

"Yeah, I guess I did. Not because I was scared to fight Wallace, though. It was because I thought we all. . . . Aw, forget it. I guess I was wrong." Greg looked up at the boys. The rawer side of their natures had taken over when there was the smell of blood. Four of them now, and not a word from them. He felt a bit sorry for them and cut the silence. "I was surprised too, Frankie. It was funny. I never expected it to come to blows. When we both got our fists up there, I couldn't believe it was happening."

"Did you expect Rich not to defend himself?" asked Carl.

"Of course not."

"You started it, Davis."

Greg sighed. "Aw, come on. . . ."

"What'd you expect?"

"I don't know, but I never expected it to go as far as it did. It was a dirty thing and it really bothers me. A fight in school. It still bothers me."

There was another long silence. Finally Frank got down to business. "Well . . . what about the team?"

"What about it?"

"Don't you care about quitting?"

"You know, since I called it quits with McKing Wednesday and had two nights sleep on it, it doesn't seem bad at all anymore."

"What'll everybody think?"

"It would do them good to think a little. Besides, look . . . just look around us. Nobody even cares."

"It hasn't come out in the school paper yet," said Henry.

"And when it does, so what? Like Rich says—and once in a while he does say something worth remembering—no-

121

body's indispensable. The team will be all right without me."

"But it's not the same as having you, Greg. We'll miss you."

"Maybe you will, Frank, because we're both juniors. But you, Danny, and you, Carl. You'll be graduating."

"Come off it, Greg," said Carl. "We still have a whole season together. We like you. You know that. And we've been on this team together for a long time now."

Greg began to feel a little sorry for his earlier flippancy. "Look. I'm sorry about giving you guys a rough time. I'm sorry for everything that's happened. But . . . but I can't say I'm sorry for what I've done, because I haven't done anything wrong. All right. So I put my fist up first. But I swear, I didn't mean to go on. You guys aren't blind. You saw what's been going on." Did he have to spell it out?

"Sure we have. And I think we all admire you for your guts and . . . and loyalty to that colored friend, Greg," said Carl. "But I still don't see why you let Rich get you down about this whole thing. I don't know how the other guys feel about it"—Carl looked around uncertainly at Danny, at Frank, at Henry—"but I think you went a little far. Heck, nobody else pays attention to Rich. Rich is just Rich, that's all." He shrugged his shoulders.

"I agree with Carl," said Frank. "To be honest, Greg, I think you're being a little . . . stubborn, quitting like this."

Greg opened his mouth to speak, but the words weren't there. They had said so many things, Carl and Frank—all of them wrong—that he didn't know just how to reply. All he could do was frown and shake his head, as though shaking it would cast up from a jumble of confused impressions the idea that was so important to make them see. But there was so much rubble to clear away first. He turned to Carl. "What do you mean . . . guts, Carl?" he said.

"Well . . . bringing a Negro around Burnside like that . . . then defending your right to do it."

That's what was wrong in the first place, thought Greg.

Jake was a thing to them—not a person, not a friend, but a nigger. And he, Greg, was a crusader who was out to change the rules. No niggers allowed, and Davis was out to break the rule. He finally spoke. "Aw, no. You're missing the shot, pals. I haven't been trying to prove anything. I haven't been showing off my guts. I just invited my friend to my home as I've invited all of you at one time or another. As for defending my right to do it, you're right about that. I'll invite anybody I want to my house any time I feel like it, and it'll take somebody bigger than Wallace to stop me. . . ."

"All right. Cool down, Greg. . . ."

"And as for Wallace . . . well . . . I think that guy is a rotton loudmouth—even if he is your girl's brother, Carl. 'Rich is Rich.' Hmph. Why is it that a guy like that always gets away with things? If any one of us acted like him, we'd be finks. But 'Rich is Rich.' Maybe if more of us told him off once in a while, he'd shape up." Greg turned to Frank. He felt especially bad about Frank's missing the point because they were both juniors and Frank had been one of his closest friends. "So you think I'm stubborn, huh, Frank?"

"Aw, I don't know, Greg. . . ."

"Well, if I'm stubborn because I can't turn my feelings on and off like a spigot when we get out on the basketball court, it's okay with me. You see, that colored boy is my friend. And it hurt. And I was mad. Now do you dig it? And I'm tired of being pushed around." It made him angrier to think that Rich Wallace could disguise himself like that, could change from his poisonous self to Burnside's popular captain as soon as he put on that blue and white uniform and pranced in front of those stupid kids and fat alumni sitting in the stands and stuffing their faces. No, nobody cared what Rich was like as long as the games were won. And maybe that was all the boys cared about, too. "So if you came here with the idea of getting me back on the team, forget it, because there's no room for Wallace and me. And I just don't feel like I belong anymore."

"Is it . . . is it that bad?" asked Frank.

"It looks that way. Sorry, Frank."

"But there have been personal feuds before, Greg," said Danny. "Don't you remember last year when Dirk and Kenny were on the outs on account of that girl?"

"Jeez!" Greg shouted. The longer they talked, the further away they became. "What's wrong with you guys? Don't you have a sense of proportion? Can't you see the hatred and tragedy that Wallace's brand of talk causes? A girl. Oh, Lord. Look. Maybe there are some principles involved. Maybe I shouldn't have apologized for looking like I had them. There's a friendship involved, but it's a matter of right and wrong, too."

The boys nodded and murmured and looked down sadly. Greg could see that he had gotten through to them in some small way. It was over, and suddenly the bell, as if in harmony with the drama, ended the scene.

"That caps it." Carl said. "Let's go. Sixth period."

"Greg and I have class together," said Frank. "I'm going to wait for him."

"Well . . . see you around, Greg," said Danny. "Take care of yourself."

"Thanks. You, too. And good luck . . . during the season."

"Thanks, Greg."

Carl stopped and turned around. "Sorry, Greg," he said.

Greg nodded.

———✐———

Greg hopped off the crosstown bus and eagerly approached the recreation center. He needed some friends now —real friends. He would kid around with Mitzi—now there was a girl! And maybe later Jake would drop by and they'd go for a hamburger. It was only at school that he was a fink, not here.

"How's our Greg?" Doc said as he entered the office.

"Fine, Doc. Uh . . . where's Mitzi?"

"She's downstairs in the craft room talking to Jake."

124

"Jake? Is he here already?"

"Yes. He's doing a paint job on those display cases. Said he couldn't work on them at home, so I told him to come on down here with them. Nobody's here early."

"Oh. So he told you about his project."

"Yep. I was talking to him yesterday. I asked him how the devil he got started on something like that and he said you pushed him into it. I want to thank you for that. I like Jake. I'd like to see him get on the beam."

Greg smiled. "I don't think you have to worry about Jake."

"He thinks a lot of you, too."

"Coming from him that's a real compliment."

"Well, you'd better go on down and relieve Mitzi. She says she's not feeling so well today, and she'd like to work outside. I thought that would be all right with you."

"Oh, sure. Sure."

Only three children were in the game room now—Dora and Cassie, the eternally-present nine-year-olds Greg always saw there, and little Alphonse Green, who was threatening to knock their game off the table. "Hi ya, Greg," the girls chorused, looking up from their parcheesi board.

"Hi, girls." He went into the arts and crafts room. Mitzi was bent over the work table talking to Jake. "Loafing, gorgeous?" he said.

"Loafing! Oh, please!" Mitzi moaned. "Mac was off today and I had to take her work, too. I think I'm coming down with a bug and Roy's coming home this weekend."

"He's gonna think we're not takin' care of you," said Jake.

"I'll take care of her," Greg growled, playfully grabbing Mitzi by the shoulders.

"Well, I think I'd like to work outside a little while," said Mitzi.

"These fumes sure ain't gonna do you no good," said Jake.

"I know. Relieve me in an hour. All right, Greg?"

"Sure thing."

125

"She's fi-i-ine," Jake droned as Mitzi walked away.

"She sure is."

"Did you meet Roy yet?"

"Her boyfriend? No."

"You're bound to one of these days. He comes by some-times."

"What are you up to here?" Greg looked at Jake's cases.

"Doc said I could work on the showcases here if I came early enough. You know what the pad's like. It's really no place to do painting. Aunt Sal was really squawkin'."

"How are the reports coming along?"

"They're in fine shape. You'll be able to type them up without a hitch. Hey, I got news."

"What?"

"Remember the one in my collection that I said I couldn't identify?"

"Little Red?"

"Yeah. Well, a couple of weeks ago, when I brought my stuff in, I showed him to Miss Hyde and she said she'd try to check him out with some people she knew. And you know what?"

"What?"

"None of 'em—and they're from the college—knew what he was." Jake beamed. "They used my notes and every-thing—bad as they were then—and told Miss Hyde they were good. Course, I polished them up since."

"Uh . . . that's good? Not knowing. . . ."

"A discovery, get it? My own discovery."

"He-ey. That's great. You'll be famous. Maybe even rich."

Jake laughed. "Naw. Nothing like that. It sure made me feel good what they said about my notes, though. Some-thing like 'gifted scientific reporting'—that's what Miss Hyde said. Eh! They'll probably find him, anyway. They're still working on it."

"Hmmm. You never know. But if he is something new, maybe they'll at least name him after you. The 'Jake Williams'. Naw, that sounds too plain. Do you have a middle name?"

"No."

"Say—what's your real name? John?"

"Maybe we just better call him the 'Jake Williams.'" Jake's eyes twinkled.

"He-ey, what are you hiding?"

"Jacques. It was Aunt Lizbeth's idea."

Greg grinned. Jake had put him in a light mood. Jake's expression now was funnier than the name, and that name on Jake was funny. They both laughed; then Jake feigned indignation.

"No kidding?" Greg said. "That's great. Say, are you busy tonight? Maybe we could celebrate your discovery. Go to the movies or something. You said the report was all right."

"Don't you have a date tonight?"

"No. The chick's busy." The Burnside Civic League was meeting at Virginia's home tonight, and her mother wanted her to be present. He was supposed to phone her after the meeting was over. "What do you say, Jake? There are lots of good movies downtown this week."

"No scratch. Spent all I had on these stains and stuff."

"It's on me. Payday today."

"Aw, no. . . ."

"Come on. I'll feel bad if you don't. I really need . . . I really feel like messing around."

"Okay, if you let me pay you back."

"When you're rich and famous. See you at a quarter to nine."

Greg came home from the movies late. They had caught the last show, and after it was over they stopped at a hangout Jake knew of downtown. It was after one—certainly too late to call Virginia. His father was still awake. "What time did Virginia call?" Greg asked him, yawning.

"She didn't call. Nobody called tonight."

"Hmmm." Greg yawned again. The meeting must have lasted late.

127

Thanksgiving always made the coming of winter easier to take. Greg rolled out of his warm bed and into the cold room. Just the thoughts of a short vacation and the special feast were worth the price of the dreary interim till Christmas. This Thanksgiving, Greg was especially grateful for the holiday. After all that had happened in the past few weeks he was getting sick and tired of going to school and seeing the same stupid and hostile people from whom he now felt so alienated. Virginia was getting on his nerves, too. Every day last week she reminded him without fail how sorry she was that he ruined things with the crowd. And she told him that somehow the story of the fight in school had leaked out to the grownups. He hoped she wouldn't get on him tonight when they went to the movies.

Today Mom was entertaining members of her family—his Aunt Martha and Uncle Jack and his cousins, Bob, Kathy and Billy. He really didn't feel like seeing relatives; his thirteen-year-old cousin Billy was a fat nuisance. He dressed and went downstairs. Already Mom had things in the oven, and wonderful odors drifted out.

Aunt Martha, Uncle Jack and the cousins came about one o'clock, and soon they were all in the living room talking and drinking.

"Are you going to do much work on your new house, Jack?" Mrs. Davis asked her brother-in-law. Uncle Jack had a small construction company.

"Just a little, Ruth. It's in pretty good shape. Only five years old. I may want to change a couple of things, build a patio in the spring. But that's about all."

"I thought you were going to build on that lot you had near the old place," said Greg's father. "That was a nice piece of property."

"Yeah . . . Well . . . I had to get out of there. The coloreds are moving in from Cole. Now, I don't have anything against

128

them, Tom, but you know what that does to property values."

Mr. Davis studied his pipe for a moment, a smile on his lips. He had heard the remark so many times.

"Aw, I know what you're thinking, Tom," Uncle Jack went on defensively. "You have your way of looking at things and I have mine. You're a social worker; I'm in property. Built that business up myself, bought that home. I can't gamble with everything. Besides," Uncle Jack grumbled, "when Betsy is Kathy's age here, you'll feel differently."

"As soon as they move into a decent house they'll be after our daughters, huh?" Mr. Davis said. Greg looked up.

"It's no joke. They keep you so busy down there trying to straighten them out, Tom, that you don't see what they're really after. But Bob tells me what goes on."

"What do you mean?"

"Some of the girls at school date colored guys," Bob explained.

Uncle Jack looked complacently at Mr. Davis; Greg's father was silent. Taking this as a concession, Uncle Jack was quick to add, "Now it's a different story, huh, Tom? Makes you see things my way, doesn't it?"

"I wouldn't say that, Jack. Whoever someone chooses to date—or even marry—isn't a simple matter of black and white—excuse the pun. It all depends on the individuals and their reasons. I don't know these people you're talking about. What do you think about it, Bob? Maybe you know some of them. You go to school there."

"They're tramps. The guys you can't blame. But the girls. . . ." Bob waved his hands in disgust.

"Do you know any of them, Bob?" Mr. Davis repeated.

"I don't have to. You can tell just be looking at them that they're no good."

"What about you, Kathy? How do you feel about it?"

"Oooo, Uncle Tom. I don't see how they could." Greg mulled over the remark. He felt compelled to grapple with it

129

in his own mind now and was disturbed that he didn't really know what he thought.

"If my sister ever did anything like that," Bob was quick to add, "I'd kick her out of the house." Kathy looked up at her brother with a worried obedience.

"Aw, look, Tom," said Uncle Jack. "We don't have anything against them. We're not against equal opportunities or anything like that. But look . . ." he bent over and lowered his voice and it turned out to be a duet—Jack and Tom Davis both said solemnly, "Would you want your daughter to marry a Negro?" Uncle Jack was startled.

"Sorry, Jack," said Mr. Davis. "I wasn't trying to be rude. But it is the classic coup de grâce . . . finish. I knew you were going to say that sooner or later."

"Well, I don't care what you call it in French. How about it?"

Greg moved closer where he could hear better. "I really couldn't say until the time came," his father answered.

"Come on now, Tom," Uncle Jack prodded.

"All right. If you want an answer now, I'll try to give you one."

"Just tell me what you think, that's all."

"Well . . . if I said yes, I'd want my daughter to marry a Negro," Mr. Davis began, "I'd be saying that I could stand to see my daughter go through a great deal of suffering at the hands of society, right?"

"C'mon, Tom. None of those tricky, ready-made answers. You know darned well what I mean so get to the point. If she didn't have to suffer and all, could you stand to see your girl married to a Negro? Do I have to spell it out?"

"No, that isn't necessary. All I can say now is if I knew my daughter wouldn't suffer and if the man had all the qualities I'd want in my daughter's husband, and I rejected him on the basis of skin color alone, then I'd have to admit that it was because of a fear or weakness inside me."

Uncle Jack sighed. "That was an awful lot of words, but I don't know if you answered the question." Even Greg wasn't sure whether it was weasling out or not; it was such an "iffy" answer.

"Well, what kind of an answer do you want? You won't take anything less than my agreeing with you . . . than admiting to being prejudiced."

"And you already did that."

"I did not. When?"

"You said you might not like it."

"Well, of course. Anything's possible."

"So with all your theories you feel just like the rest of us that the Negro is something else."

"Oh, no. I never said anything like that. I don't think there's anything wrong with the Negro. I do think there's something wrong with most white people on this whole point, though. And that something is ignorance. Lack of self-knowledge."

"What do you mean?"

"We don't know ourselves—just what I said. We don't know what makes us tick. And some of what we do know we don't like. So we say it's not there."

"Riddles yet. Like what?"

"This whole problem of mixed marriage is full of things that hit hard—sex, guilt, pressures from the outside, status. We don't like to admit it, but most of us have to have someone to be better than. The Negro is a sitting duck. What would we do without him?"

"Well, we are. . . ."

"We don't like to admit it, but we're scared to death of what other people think. We're so scared that, if someone puts the pressure on, we'll throw anybody to the lions. Look what happened to the people under the Nazis. Well, that's another story."

"Aw . . . I don't know. I just don't know," said Uncle Jack. "But you guys with the books. Sometimes you sound like you flipped your wigs. All full of words and theories that just don't have anything to do with the facts. Somebody spits in your eye and you call it rain. You don't understand, so you

131

try to make things up. You talk this whole different language, that us plain people down here don't even understand."

"Then what are the facts, Jack?"

"I. . . ." Uncle Jack was silent for a long time. "I don't know."

Greg stared at his uncle. All that questioning and answering and picking things to pieces, and old Uncle Jack couldn't come back with anything better than that lost "I don't know."

"You see," Mr. Davis said, "by making this whole business of mixed marriage sound like a repulsive thing, people deny their own attraction to the idea. Also, they have a scapegoat and can eliminate competition for jobs and mates. Then the rest of the people are scared to be different, to buck the whole set-up. That's why that question—"Would you want your daughter . . . or sister . . . to marry a Negro?"—carries so much punch. A man who doesn't want his daughter to marry a Negro—whatever his reasons—gets conned into supporting all kinds of discrimination. He's bluffed by the hard-core bigots into thinking that any gain the Negro makes in the way of education or improving his condition is just a step toward getting a white girl—as though that were the Negro's only goal."

"Dad?" said Greg.

"Yes, Greg?"

"You know all this. Yet you admitted that you might still object to . . . to Betsy's marrying a Negro. Why do you feel that way?"

"That's what I asked him in the first place," grumbled Uncle Jack.

"With me I guess it's a matter of aesthetics."

"Now what the hell's that?"

"Jack!" scolded Aunt Martha. "Don't be rude."

"It's a matter of what we think is beautiful and why. But it's much more than that, because what we do like or don't like, on the surface, is tied up with all the tricky things we've been talking about. That's the reason for the hundred-dollar word. If you don't like that word, Jack, you could call it taste."

"Taste!" shouted Uncle Jack.

"Taste?" Greg echoed.

"You mean like blondes, brunettes, redheads, fat ones, skinny ones?" said Uncle Jack. "And now black ones and white ones?"

"Something like that."

"You're talking off the top of your head again, Tom. You're talking so much off the top of your head that you're telling your guts lies."

"Like I said, it's tied up with a lot of other things. I had pretty much the same background as you on this score, Jack. And I'll admit, I might be afraid of what other people would say."

"So after driving around the long way again, you're still the same as we are."

"No, Jack. There's one very important difference."

"What's that?"

"I might not be able to cross the color line myself, but if someone I knew did, I wouldn't be ready to lynch the Negro. And that's what counts."

"Except if it was your daughter."

"You're trying to put words in my mouth again, Jack. I didn't say that. You did. You're the one who's so sure I'd go to pieces. I said I might. But then, the ceiling might fall down on us today. In fact, I'd be willing to bet that if mixed marriages were commonplace by the time Betsy grew up, I wouldn't be too upset if she married a worthwhile Negro. Right now, I'd be afraid of her . . . us . . . being 'different.' "

"I can't believe you'd say a thing like that, Tom. I wouldn't spread it around if I was you, either."

"I know. People don't like doubters. It makes them realize they could be wrong."

"I bet you're the only white person who thinks like that."

"Far from it. In some parts of the world there are people who are color-blind. They're more than free from prejudice; they simply don't care about color much at all. I think it's largely in our own country and Africa that people get so upset."

"Well, you never know what those foreigners are gonna do anyway; they've been corrupted by wars and stuff. But that's a lot of baloney you're trying to pass around today."

Mr. Davis shrugged his shoulders. "You can take it or leave it. I know it all sounds strange, but it is strange. It's not the kind of truth people go looking for. It was strange to me once, too. But it's the only thing anybody's been able to come up with. And it takes a long time to sink in, so there's no point in talking about it anymore. Did you watch the Giants last Sunday?" And the conversation turned to sports.

"Did you walk over today?" Greg asked as Jake hopped up on the curb at their meeting place on Saturday afternoon.

"Not today, man. Not me. I don't dig this cold weather at all. And it looks like it's gonna rain."

"Then why were you coming from that direction? And the crosstown bus just passed."

"Oh. I stopped in your drugstore—you know that one—to get this pack of typing paper. Didn't even think you might need it till the last minute when I was already on the bus, so I went there."

"Oh. I have plenty at home. That's a pretty fat stack of papers you have there."

"Yeah. I've been workin' hard since I saw you last Sunday. And with Thanksgiving and all, I got a lot done. I feel kinda bad about putting you through all this work, Greg. I know you're busy. Jan can type, but she don't know much about writin' this all up slick."

"It's all right. I scheduled it in."

"Don't know how you can do it, Davis, workin' and basketball and all. Hey, wait a minute! How come you were at work yesterday instead of being at that Carlisle game?"

"Oh . . . I'm . . . uh . . . not playing ball anymore. There's a full practice schedule now, and I decided the job was more important. How did you know about the game?"

"I was reading the scores in the morning paper."

"Who won?"

"You cats took it from Carlisle."

"Good." Greg pushed his fists up over his head and stretched contentedly. Then he froze stupidly in that position. Some boys across the street—Rich Wallace and a couple of seniors Greg didn't know too well. His heart began to beat faster. It was nothing but an unlucky coincidence; what else? Mc-Ginnis' drugstore . . . Skippy . . . He felt a sense of dread as they began to cross over. They had seen him and they had wanted to see him; he could tell. What were they up to? How should he act?

His mind blanked and the next thing he knew Rich was right there, no more than a foot away from him, his warm breath stifling Greg's own as he spoke. "Going somewhere, Davis?"

"Y-yeah," Greg stammered. Rich, wordless, glared into Greg's eyes. "Home," Greg added stupidly.

"Then you'd better get moving, huh, Davis?" Greg stared. Rich moved even closer and wedged himself between Greg and Jake. "Come on, Davis. Let's go."

Greg stiffened, meeting the resistance of Rich's hard body.

"C'mon, Davis. . . ."

Greg tightened his fists. His eyes took in Rich's shoulders and he imagined how good it would feel to grab and throw him. The bus they had been waiting for sped by.

"Let's go, Davis."

Greg saw Jake's puzzled brown eyes just above Rich's head. "Don't pay any attention, Jake. Let's walk. . . ."

"Not you, nigger," Rich muttered. "You just go back

where you came from." His rosy neck and square jaw were bared as he glanced over his shoulder.

Greg—enraged, hurt—savagely crashed his fist into the bone, rammed his knuckles in under the soft flesh, and forced him back into Jake.

But Rich recovered quickly, and his fist cut into Greg's cheek, forcing him to blink his eyes and topple back.

Greg lunged back in desperation. Now he felt wild with rage. It wasn't like the first time. He pounded and pounded. He wanted to knock the very life out of Rich, to beat him till he was a weak, limp rag who would shake in his grip.

But Rich was strong, and his fists beat soundly on Greg's body, on his face, his shoulders, his chest. . . .Greg was down, and using all the strength he had to hold his head from crashing onto the pavement while Rich battered his face. He gasped and began to sob.

The two boys had Jake close up against a parked car. "Get outta' here, black boy."

"Go back where you came from unless you wanna get the same."

Jake ploughed through them and ran over and grabbed Rich by the shoulders with his two large brown hands and began pulling him off. Greg strained with all his might at the break and got away from Rich for a second. But the two boys came behind Jake. Jake wheeled; with a swift swing of his arms he chopped both boys across the face and Greg saw a tumble of arms and legs as Jake took them on. We've gotta stop, he thought. . . . But Rich came at him again and Greg drew strength desperately, slugging at his shoulders until Rich was pinned against a car in front of the house. "Had . . . enough, Wallace?" Ungh. "Gonna let me . . . alone?" Another punch. "Huh?" Greg drew a deep breath and hit him again.

Suddenly the sound of a screaming siren was heard and a patrol wagon stopped by the curb. Jake had one boy's arm twisted behind him and the other boy by the back of the neck. Two police officers slid out of the car. The front door of a nearby house banged open and a stocky middle-aged lady toddled out in bedroom slippers screaming, "There they are! That's them!"

"We're not blind, lady," one of the policemen said.

"All right boys. Let's all take a little ride down to number fifteen and talk it over," said the other.

"I don't think. . . ." Rich Wallace gasped, "I don't think . . . that will be . . . necessary."

"Izzat so?" said one of the officers. "Well, we'll see. Now. . . ."

"I think . . . everyone will agree that . . . the best thing to do is go home quietly."

"Izzat a fact?" the policeman said, raising his eyebrows. "What's your name, sonny?"

"That won't be necessary, officer."

"You like to give orders, don't you, sonny? Now suppose you get in the car with the rest of the boys, and we'll talk it over at the station."

The other policeman was talking to the woman. "We getcha, Missus. You don't know who started it. But you'll still have to come down and tell us what you saw since it was you who called us. It won't cause any trouble for you."

Everyone in the wagon was silent, except for the woman who whined, "Never had anything like this in Burnside. Ooooo! Never had riots in Burnside before. Isn't any place decent to live in these days?"

Greg felt like crying every time he glanced sideways at Jake staring stonefaced before him. Greg couldn't stand to look at Rich, but down inside somewhere he felt a hot, excited, violently happy satisfaction that he was being dragged along in the car with his mouth clamped shut.

The station wasn't very far from where the fight had taken place, and soon Greg was sitting across from one of the policemen giving him routine information about his name, age, where he went to school, his father's name, father's occupation. "A social worker's kid? That's a hot one!" the policeman said and took down his address and telephone number. "All

137

right, son," the officer said, "just have a seat till your father comes. And . . . there's a room in back. Go wash off your face."

"My father? Aw, why . . . ?"

"Next!" The police officer motioned to Jake.

Greg lingered near the desk as Jake went through the same routine. "What are you doing up here, Williams?" the officer asked. Why did a policeman have to say that? thought Greg. Why couldn't he come up here like anybody else? Jake was looking worriedly at the desk and did not answer. "Eh?" the officer prodded.

"He came up to visit me," Greg said. "We're working. . . ."

"The boy's got a mouth."

"Came up to see Greg about some school work," Jake said slowly.

"Oh yeah? What are ya studyin'? Karate?"

"He tried to break it up," Greg said quickly.

"Not the way he was swingin' when my eyes saw 'im. Now go wash that mess off your face. We'll hear what you have to say about it, boy," the police officer said to Jake.

And Jake quietly told him where he was going, and how the boys, whom he had never seen before, started to insult them. "Greg was takin' a bad beatin', and I didn't want to see him take no beatin' on my account," he explained sadly.

"So you thought you'd make it two to one, huh?"

"That's not true, officer," said Greg, and the man glared angrily.

"Didn't mean it that way. No, sir," said Jake.

"He tried to break it up," Greg insisted.

"One more word outta you, sonny, and we'll put you in the pokey where you won't bother anybody. Now go wash that face before your mother gets here and has a fit; then sit tight! You, too, Williams. Sit down till your people come. Next! You!" The policeman motioned to Rich Wallace.

Greg was appalled when he looked into the small mirror above the washbasin in the back room and saw the purple crust between his nose and mouth on the right side of his face. His own blood. Ugh! His cheek was an angry red that he knew would be turning blue. And that eye. . . . When he came out of the washroom he saw his father sitting by Jake and talking. He saw Jake say a few words. Good. He was glad Dad had arrived.

The boys had given their vital statistics and other information and sat waiting for their parents and for the police captain. Rich and his two cronies were on the opposite side of Greg, his father, and Jake. Mr. Davis was expectant but calm and did not seem to want to talk much right then and there. The lady who had phoned the police sat nervously huddled in a corner.

Soon Mr. Wallace came. He stomped right over to Rich, ignoring everyone else, pushed back his hat and shouted, "What are you doing down here?" Rich began muttering to his father. The room was silent enough but it was big; Greg strained his ears, but it was to no avail. He could only sit back helplessly as he watched Rich mutter and nod over at them, and soon Mr. Wallace turned and gave Jake a long, cold stare. Soon, the other white boys' parents arrived and joined them, and eventually, the captain entered.

Aunt Sallie was the last to arrive. She appeared at the doorway and stood still for the longest time. An old black coat stretched tautly over her ample body; her legs looked like two smoked hams; and on her feet, which pointed this way and that, were gargantuan brown moccasins. Everyone sat gaping while she stood there stock-still, her thick, rock-like head rolling from side to side, her black eyes looking around suspiciously and fearfully. Finally she walked straight up to the captain's desk, merely glancing at Jake.

The captain motioned for everyone to assemble before the bench and asked the police officers to report.

"This lady here phoned us and told us a gang of boys was fighting in front of her house. When we pulled up all these boys here were goin' to town, so we can't say who started it. This one," he continued, jutting his chin in the direction of

Greg, "admits he took the first punch, but that don't necessarily mean he's all to blame, least as far as I'm concerned." The other officer nodded in agreement. "The discrep'ncy comes as to how this one"—he indicated Jake—"joined the party. His friend claims he wanted to break it up; the other boys claim he jumped this Wallace fella, which is a horse of a different color."

"All right, Cranston," said the captain. "The boys will tell it themselves from here on in."

When Rich went over his story, he said, "I was fighting. With Davis here. I admit it. But then this . . . guy jumped me," he added, giving Jake a dirty look.

"That's a lie!" hollered Greg.

"All right, sonny. You'll get your turn," said the captain.

"I don't have the habit of getting into street fights, sir," Wallace went on coolly. "If you'd let us all go home, it won't happen again."

"We'll see, sonny. This is my precinct," said the captain. "I'll do what I think is best."

Rich's two cronies backed up his story, saying that they tried to pull Jake off when he began beating Rich in an uneven fight.

"My Jake ain't no troublemaker!" Aunt Sallie suddenly shouted. "He may be on the dumb side at times, but he ain't no troublemaker 'n never was. I tried to warn him that there was no profit in messin' around with white people, and jus' look—he was never in a po-lice station till he went and did. . . ."

"All right, Miss Williams, calm down. Nobody said he was a troublemaker. I don't think we can say anything one way or another because no one saw the whole thing. We're just glad that Officers Cranston and Dobbs got there before anyone got hurt and before any damage was done to Mrs. Huff's property. Now you all look like decent people to me, and we don't have any records on the boys. We'll keep it that way, all right? Now you folks take the boys home and talk to them—I think you know what's at the heart of this." The

140

captain swung around and stepped down; no one seemed to have anything more to say.

Mr. Wallace was the first to make a move. "Let's get out of here," he snarled to Rich; then, as he brushed by Greg's father, "I'd advise you to keep your kid in line, Mr. Davis."

"Would you mind explaining that?"

"Yes. I'll explain, Mr. Davis. If he were my kid, I'd knock him around before somebody else did. And right now there are a lot of people who'd like to get the chance."

"My son did nothing wrong."

"Look, Mr. Davis. If he can't pick the right friends, that's your problem. But don't get the rest of us involved in his tricks."

"I don't see where he bothered anyone."

"We want our streets white and our stores white. And our homes white. If you don't want it that way, you can move out of Burnside. I'll see if I can provide you with some funds. If you don't get the point after today, Mr. Davis, I don't know what it's going to take. But we'll find something." He nudged his son forward and they left.

"What a. . . . The nerve of that guy!" Greg exclaimed. "Why'd you just stand there, Dad? Why did you let him talk to you that way? Why didn't you tell him off?"

"There's nothing I could tell him that wouldn't take half a lifetime, Greg. You might as well try to forget this whole thing."

Greg grabbed Jake by the arm. "You hear that, Jake? Come on, let's get to work and forget this ever happened."

"Can't just do that, Davis. Didn't know all this was happening to you. Can't just forget."

"You just get yourself home where you belongs," grumbled Aunt Sallie. "You disgraced yo'self enough in front of this trash. I ain't so old I can't kick you around some yet."

"Let Jake come up with us as he planned, Miss Williams," said Greg's father. "The boys are working. . . ."

"Ain't none of yo' business, mistuh."

"Can I give you a ride home?"

"I'll go back the way I came, thank you," Aunt Sallie said curtly. "And I'll take this fool heah with me." She pulled Jake by the arm and out the door.

"That's a pretty nasty cut you have on your face," Greg's father said in the car on the way home.

"Yeah. I hate to let Mom . . . Dad!"

"What's the matter?"

"The papers!"

"What?"

"Jake's papers. His report for the contest. I . . . don't remember seeing him carrying them out when he left the station. And I . . . I. . . ." Greg buried his head in his hands. He couldn't bear to think of what might have happened to them by now. "I didn't see him pick them up when the cops came. Dad . . . please . . . we've got to go back and look."

"Where?" said Mr. Davis. "What papers?"

"Jake's report is all over the street! Don't ask questions. Just hurry. Corner of Harper and Amity." Wordlessly, Mr. Davis swung the car in the opposite direction. "Oh, God. Please let them be there."

Mr. Davis had hardly stopped the car before Greg slid out, trembling with relief. About half of the papers were still by the parked car where Jake had dropped them and the rest were scattered and trampled in front of Mrs. Huff's hedge.

In the car he held the papers almost tenderly on his lap. It was raining now. It pained him to see pages that were torn and scuffed—it was a sad testimony to the weeks of work and hope of one of the nicest guys he had ever known. Greg felt sick when he remembered the stunned, strange look on Jake's face and the way Jake had refused to look at him. Then he looked back down at the papers and felt a little hope. Somehow, if he had these, he still had Jake in his grip.

At home his mother choked back tears as she applied antiseptic and ice packs to Greg's bruises. Mr. Davis had already given her a long, calm explanation of what had happened;

neither parent had doubted the truth of Greg's story for a moment. "Why are people so mean?" she said.

Just before dinner Greg muttered, "It's about time I called Virginia."

"Oh, Greg, why don't you just stay home tonight?" his mother said. "Hasn't it been enough for one day?"

"I have to call her anyway. Besides, I feel like I could use a little fun right now."

The phone rang for a long time before Mrs. Ashburn answered it. She sounded irritated. "Oh . . . it's you, Greg. What is it you want?"

What the heck did she think he wanted, Greg thought. It certainly wasn't to talk to her. "I'd like to speak to Virginia," he said.

"She's ill."

"Can't . . . can't I talk to her?"

"No. I mean . . . she's resting now. We . . . she doesn't want to be disturbed."

"Well . . . I'll call back later, then. About tonight."

"How can she go out if she's ill?" Mrs. Ashburn snapped.

"I. . . . What's wrong, Mrs. Ashburn?"

"Greg, please don't call here again." Click. The hum of an idle line.

Greg's heart was in his throat. He knew darned well what was wrong. You didn't keep a story like today's quiet very long, not with all the acquaintances Mrs. Ashburn had. Still nobody, no human being, deserved that kind of treatment. She had treated him like dirt. Hadn't even asked him how he was or what his side of the story was. What manners, the ignorant old. . . . And she thought she was one of the gracious ladies of Burnside. In a pig sty.

He didn't care about her anyway. It was Virginia who was on his mind. Why hadn't she come to the phone? And that story about being sick. Was it her idea? He didn't dare call her home again . . . But yes, he would call back. Late. He'd call back when there was barely enough time to get dressed and go out. Then Virginia would have to put her cards on the table, would have to tell him whether or not she wanted to see him, and knowing how she was about Saturday night dates. . . .

He phoned again at seven-thirty. Nobody answered.

Greg felt trapped and lonely. He felt he had to go out; to forget, to defy some mysterious someone or something that was trying to shut him out of things. He wished there were someone with whom he could laugh and cut up everybody and everything. But there was nobody. They had even driven Jake away. He would have to call him, too. He wondered how it would be. And consoled himself with the idea that it might be good for him to have to sit home and face things instead of running away. He'd work on Jake's report, so that tomorrow he could tell him how good it was and that now it was in fine shape.

———

On Sunday Greg awoke to a dazzling morning sun. The numbness of his bruises had subsided but his face gave him a painful reminder of the Saturday just gone by. As he came down for breakfast, he saw the telephone at the bottom of the stairs. Black monster. He hoped that yesterday's urge to contact Virginia wouldn't revive and spoil the day with suspicions and disappointments. Sick or not sick? Hmph. The lady or the tiger. The phone call he would have to make to Jake would be hard enough. Soon he was in the kitchen getting some solace from a big weekend breakfast.

His mother called into the kitchen. "Telephone, Greg. It's Virginia. Should I tell her you're eating?"

"Virginia?" Greg ran to the phone and grabbed the receiver. "He-ey, what's happening?"

"I can't talk, Greg. I've got to hurry. I'm at church and I managed to get away for a minute. I just wanted to tell you not to call today. I'll talk to you in school tomorrow."

"What . . . what's the matter?"

"I can't talk now," Virginia said and hung up.

Now Greg really felt bothered. The whole day ruined, he thought, and it's hardly begun. What was coming off anyway? He was glad he still had Jake's papers to type. At least it gave him something to do and it didn't involve thinking.

When Greg phoned Jake late that afternoon, he was relieved to hear the pleasant voice of Jake's father. It gave him a chance to brace himself for Jake. Luckily Chubby Williams hadn't even asked who was calling and Aunt Sallie hadn't answered the phone.

Then Jake was there. "Hello?"

"Jake? Greg."

There was a silence; then Jake said simply, "Hi, Greg."

"I . . . I got some news."

"Yeah?" Jake said lifelessly.

"Uh-huh. Your report. I finished it. Typing it, I mean. I . . . I managed to get through it all my myself. Good, huh?" Sounds, sounds, Greg thought nervously, clenching and unclenching his fist; it wasn't like they were talking at all. He was sputtering into an instrument, and Jake was a machine that uttered "uh-huhs." "Looks good to me," Greg went on. "I mean, I don't know much about it, but. . . ." This couldn't go on. He knew Jake long enough now to realize that when Jake was like this—quiet, sullen, lost—the best thing to do was to lambaste him, to put it straight and strong and tell him to come out with it. "What's the matter with you today, Jake? You sound like you're half dead."

Jake still said nothing, but Greg had the feeling that he might have jolted him from his stupor.

"And what was the big idea leaving those papers all over the street yesterday?" Greg went on. Still no answer. "Huh?" he prodded.

"I forgot them."

"Forgot?? What if I hadn't remembered them?"

"I don't know. . . ."

"What if I hadn't remembered them, huh?" Greg said again, this time to himself as well as to Jake. The idea made him shiver now. It was a miracle that he had noticed their absence in all the misery of the day past. He had been stupid not to call Jake last night and reassure him. "Weren't you worried about them? Didn't you go back?"

"No."

"Why not?"

"It kinda seemed the end of things."

"What do you mean?"

"I didn't know you were having trouble on account of me."

"Do you think I care about those goons we met yesterday?"

"There's more to it than yesterday. You can't fool me, Davis."

"What kind of a guy do you think I am?"

"You don't owe me anything."

"No. I don't. And I never did anything for you that was any skin off my nose, either. Don't think that. I have everything I could want. And I still do. And I still don't see what this has to do with your leaving your biology report all over the street."

"Just a feeling, I guess. You been with me from the beginning of the project, and I guess I had you all connected up with it. When you were getting that beating yesterday, it seemed like the end of everything."

"That's the stupidest thing I ever heard. All that work. Did you think you were paying me for those lumps? Did you think you were punishing yourself by . . . by chucking everything you've done?"

"Something like that."

Greg sighed. "Well, I'm glad that's all straightened out. Now we can get back to normal. Thank God I salvaged. . . ."

But Jake wasn't finished. "Never been insulted like that before," he said coldly.

It seemed like a challenge, an accusation against him, in fact, and Greg automatically apologized. But then he became angry. He had been tricked. He had been tricked into shouldering the burden of guilt, just because it was he who

146

had pierced Jake's ghetto fortress. "So you've never been insulted that way before," he shouted. "Big deal. Don't stand up and you won't get slapped down. Go on. Hide down there in Cole and lick your wounds with Aung Sallie and Lester and everybody else. Then nobody will bother you. Eat your chitt'lins. Maybe you want to forget the science fair, too. After all, the judges are probably ofays, too. I'll just throw these papers in the rubbish. . . ."

"No! I . . . I'm sorry, Greg. I was just punchin' out at the wrong man. I'm really sorry."

"Well, do you want me to drive them down tonight?"

"Don't go through no trouble. I'll be at practice same as usual on Tuesday."

"Well . . . I'd really like to get out of the house for a little while, Jake. And this way you can show it to Miss Hyde tomorrow and you won't lose two days. All right?"

"Aunt Sal's home."

"Well, meet me down on the corner. At seven. We'll go for a coke someplace."

———⚍———

Virginia, who had fourth period gym on the same floor as the cafeteria, was in the front of the lunch line. After paying the cashier, she did not go to their regular spot where some of the other juniors sat. When Greg came out of the line he found her in the farthermost corner of the cafeteria by a group of seventh grade girls. They ogled him as he sidestepped over to her. He was glad he would be settling things with her, too, but it all looked so ominous.

"Well, me lovely," he said lightly, trying to cover his mounting nervousness, "what strange secrets are we sharing today? Or am I exiled now?"

"Well . . . I just thought we ought to talk about it privately."

"Talk about what?" Greg said.

"You know. The weekend."

"All right. Out with it. Why couldn't I see you? Or even talk to you? Did you have measles or something?"

"I wasn't sick, Greg," Virginia answered softly.

"To hear your mother talk, I thought you were dying."

"She was lying."

"That's obvious. Why?"

"She didn't want me to see you."

"That's pretty obvious, too. Why?"

Virginia started to speak, but hesitated. "That's pretty obvious, too, isn't it, Greg?" she finally said.

"You mean the fight?"

Virginia nodded.

"J-Jeez, Virginia. How about hearing my side of the story?"

"I don't have to hear it, Greg. Knowing you and Rich; I'm sure it wasn't your fault or your friend's."

"Well listen anyway," Greg demanded, and as he told her beginning from the time Jake had stopped in McGinnis' till the time they were fighting on the street, Virginia nodded and kept nodding; she understood perfectly.

"I know, I know. I believe your story and I understand. But don't you see? With Mother and the people in the Civic League, it doesn't matter. They made up their minds about you and your friend a long time ago. Saturday only gave them an excuse, something to point to. . . ."

"Wait! What? The Civic League? Where do they come in?"

Virginia sighed. "I told you about it. They were talking about you last week. Even before the fight Saturday."

"What for?"

"That . . . colored boy."

"What about him?"

"It's just that you've been so close with him. They can't understand why you'd do a thing like that. . . ."

"Do what??"

"Well, let me finish!"

"Go ahead."

"They can't understand why you'd have to bring a colored person around, give him ideas, when you have so many nice friends from school."

"I don't have a friend in the whole pack."

"That's your problem, Greg."

"And why can't I let him walk around here? I've seen other Negroes. Their houseboys. The boys who cut their grass and landscape their yards. Or don't I 'keep him in his place'? Is that what's wrong?"

"They just can't understand you, Greg. They said things like . . . like 'if you associate with trash you must be trash yourself.'"

"Jeez!" A crazy smile tugged at the corner of Greg's mouth. It was all too trite. For the longest time he just sat with his cheese sandwich in his hand and stared at Virginia, thinking how absurd it all was. They might have said he was a dirty boy or had pimples or something. It was an old, old story. He thought of the Civic Leaguers he knew—Henry Johnson's parents, John McGinnis and his daughter, Mrs. Bryce, Mrs. Wallace. That was enough. And Mrs. Ashburn always did strike him as a gutless person who could be told where to turn. They had probably put the screws on her, all right. The victim of a bunch of sheep, he thought angrily. "So tell me more gore, doll. What else happened last week, before the vultures got their big chance?"

"Well . . . when Mrs. Wallace came, she looked at me in a snotty way and told Mom she wanted to talk to her alone when they got the chance. Later I saw them sneaking off into Mom's room—I was so nervous I watched them all night—and I went by the door. I couldn't get too much. It was mostly whispers, but they were talking about us, all right, and naturally, something about Negroes. I heard them mention John McGinnis and something about giving people ideas. That's when I found out they knew about the school fight. Rich's mother said something about spoiling his good name. . . ."

"What a phony! That guy's rotten."

149

"And that maybe I could talk to you. So I did. Don't say I didn't warn you, Greg," said Virginia.

"Warn me? Warn me! You have a lot of nerve!"

"Well, if you're going to shout at me, why go through all the trouble of asking me questions?"

"All right. Go on. Then what happened?"

"Well . . . even then, Mother was upset. She said. . . . She said . . . Oh. . . ."

"What did she say?"

"She said . . . why did I have to . . . go out with you. She said . . . there were a lot of nice boys at school."

"Nice boys? Then what does that make me?"

"Well, after the street fight on Saturday. . . . That was IT, Greg. Whoever called her said you were a troublemaker."

It was a name slippery enough to stick and for everyone to use. A troublemaker. Of course, thought Greg. Perfect. They couldn't say Virginia shouldn't see him because he had a Negro friend, brought him to his house and everything, brought him into their nice, vanilla-white ice cream parlors. No. The League people would be the last ones to admit to such undisguised prejudice. It was downright un-American, unfashionable. But—Greg brings Negroes who make trouble? The kind who fight with their sons on the streets? A different matter—if you wanted to believe there was a difference.

Greg felt helpless and lost. There was no more arguing about the Burnside League. As far as they were concerned, they had a closed case. "So. What do you think about all this, Virginia?"

"I . . . I don't know."

"You don't know? A girl's mother stops her from seeing a guy because she doesn't like the color of his friend's skin, and a bunch of snobs and phonies smear a guy behind his back because they don't like it either, and 'you don't know'?"

"Well, I never said they were right about this, Greg. And I never said you were wrong."

"Wha . . . What kind of an answer is that?" Greg asked. "What are you saying, then? Say it."

"Well . . . what do you want me to talk about? About . . . your friend? The fights? About going with you?"

"Don't act dumb, Virginia. You know they're all part of the same mess."

"Don't make me nervous!" The girl sat frowning, searching for words. "Well," she finally began, "the kids admire you for doing what you think is right. We admire the way you've stood up to Rich. And . . . in spite of our personal feelings, we admire your lack of prejudice. . . ."

"We admire". . . . "We admire". . . . The words ground and ground into Greg's brain like a broken record. Soon he wasn't even hearing her words. All he knew was that some collective "we" was secretly passing judgment again, and like the members of the team that day in the cafeteria, they had completely missed the point. She might as well have been saying, befriend, defend whatever things you please; Jake was just an issue to her, too. Right now she sounded like he had acted creepy at one of their parties and she was tolerating him. "Stop, Virginia," he finally said. "Don't say anymore."

"What's wrong?"

"Everything, Virginia."

"I don't understand."

He forced an ironical laugh. "That's what's wrong. You don't understand. Well, let me explain. I'm not on trial here, Virginia. And I'm not interested in hearing what kind of judgment this 'we' you're talking about is making. If you're talking about your gang, I don't care what they admire anymore. They're a bunch of block-heads, even if they are patting me on the back. So let's get to the point. Are you going to keep seeing me?"

"Am I . . . am I supposed to disobey my mother?"

Greg dropped his head in exaggerated exasperation. "Oh, no. Let's cut the dutiful daughter act."

"What do you mean?"

"I mean, I've never known you to worry about what your parents said when there was something you wanted to do. Like cruise around Bedford."

"Well . . . this is different."

"How?"

"Well . . . those other things you're referring to. She didn't know about them."

"You could see me around if you wanted to. You know that."

"It . . . it would be so hard. I don't want any more trouble with my family."

"So what are you going to do?"

"All this has been making me very nervous, Greg. My nerves have been very bad lately. . . ."

"The 'Nervous Wreck' game."

"Stop it! It's all your fault anyway."

"Mine? Why?"

"You had to go and . . . and . . ."

"What?"

"You had to go and . . . make an oddball out of yourself. Everything was so nice. We had fun, we did things, we went places, had lots of friends, and you had to go ahead and mess it up." She went on, wondering why Greg had to get the job, why he had met Jake. "Why did this have to happen?"

"Virginia . . . it might never have happened. But it did. And I think it was a good thing. For me, at least. But everything else that's followed has been bad. They're wrong. You know they are, Virginia. So why go on wishing it all away and blaming me? Stop lying to yourself and to me. Tell me the truth, Virginia. Tell me how you honestly feel and I promise I won't say a word. No matter what the truth is."

"All right." The girl sighed but didn't speak for a long time. "I guess . . . the truth is . . . I'm selfish. I'm ready to admit it now. I know I'm only going to be young once. I have my own troubles, and right now, I don't want anybody else's. The way I see it, Greg, I've got plenty of time to crusade in my life and worry about serious things when I'm older. Right now I want to have fun. I don't see why I should have to give it up. I . . . I don't hurt anybody. Have I hurt anybody, Greg? No. I'm not a saint, but I don't hurt anybody, either. Isn't that enough?"

Greg shook his head but the words couldn't come right out. "Jeez, I don't know, Virginia. I used to think it was. But somehow it's not. Not when you know somebody . . . a person who's getting the dirty end of it. . . ."

"Well, if that's not good enough for you, I'm sorry. It's the best I can do." Virginia looked up, and Greg was surprised to see her eyes filled with tears. He was too hurt to say anything. She spoke again. "I guess . . . I sound pretty awful, Greg. I . . . I'm sorry."

"Well at least you've been honest about it."

"I'm bothered by this, Greg," Virginia looked up. "I really am. Don't think I'm not."

"Sure, sure."

"I really am, Greg. And I've got to think about this. I have to do it alone. By myself. Without anybody pushing me. Do you understand what I'm saying?"

"I read you, doll." A lump was in his throat. "I guess I need to be alone, too. I've got to work things out without other people getting involved. I've got to think, too."

The tears streamed down her cheeks and Greg touched her hand. He felt like crying, too. They had been going together for almost seven months, the longest he had gone with any one girl. She was so pretty. He remembered their first date, right at the beginning of spring. It was on Founder's Day. She had danced in the assembly program, and that evening they went to a semi-formal and she wore a lavendar dress. They dated all summer, and now . . . there wouldn't be any more dates with Virginia Ashburn. . . .

The bell whirred. "Oh, Greg," she said. "I don't want to go."

"We have to."

"Greg. I'll see you tonight. I'll meet you at Rex's."

Greg was ready to say yes, but he remembered some of the things that had happened. "I don't know, Virginia. We've been on different wave lengths, lately. I don't think we should."

"Oh, Greg. Just think. If you hadn't started that job. . . . Any other recreation center. . . ."

"No. Don't say that. Don't say any more that you'll be sorry for. See what I mean? It's better that we all had the chance to. . . ." To what? he thought. ". . . to find out what we're really like. . . . We can't go back together now. We'll just lie to each other about our feelings. There's been enough lying, Virginia."

The girl, worn from crying, sighed and nodded.

"We'd better go, Virginia. We're almost late for class."

"Good-by, Greg," Virginia said and ran out of the empty cafeteria. The tables clean, the busboys were stacking the stools.

Greg walked slowly to his history class. He felt heartsick, but in her confusion Virginia had revealed something to him. Her confusion had been the signs of guilt, denial and ignorance. Maybe there was hope. Maybe they all felt the same—the Burnside Civic League, the kids at school—confused and guilty, realizing that somehow they were wrong. Yet their consciences were trapped by this unknown thing. What was it? Was it fear of each other?

He felt . . . luckier, wiser. He was free of this thing, whatever it was. He was no longer a pariah.

DISCOVERY

Greg finished what he had to say about the History Club's exhibit for Activities Night; there was no more business and the weekly meeting adjourned early. Greg checked his watch. Almost ten minutes left of last period, so there would be no rush. Mr. Garsky was coming up to the front of the room now. He walked up slowly, a friendly smile on his face. "You want to see me about something, Greg?" he said.

"Yes, sir. I finally have some ideas for that semester paper," said Greg.

"Oh, yes."

Greg pulled up a chair for the teacher and sat down himself. "Well," he began, "I'd like to do something a little different. There's something I'd like to look into very much, and to be honest, I don't have any other ideas besides this one. But I don't know how to work it in with Problems of Democracy."

"What is it?"

"Prejudice."

"What do you have in mind?"

"Well . . . I've been wondering what makes people prejudiced . . . what prejudice really is, so I thought that this would kill two birds with one stone. I'm . . . uh . . . late getting started on this paper, as you know, but I'd really like to do some reading on the subject."

"I see," Mr. Garsky said, smiling. "I'm . . . uh . . . aware of your recent adventures with the basketball team."

Greg reddened; he wondered just how much Mr. Garsky did know. It would be easier to talk now. "You see, Mr. Garsky, after all this happened, and I spent some time thinking about it, the thought struck me that all these people— except one, maybe—were like prisoners of something they didn't understand. They'd say things like, 'I know I'm wrong. I don't know why. But I just can't help it.' And they'd let it go at that. Do you see what I mean?"

"Yes. Yes, I can see what must have struck you—the mystery about the whole phenomenon, and, at the same time, the grip it had."

"That's right."

"So you want to satisfy your own curiosity about what it is?"

"Well . . . not only that," Greg said defensively. He had been afraid of something like this, that the topic wouldn't be suitable for the course. "I mean, prejudice is a problem of democracy and I thought that discovering its nature might point the way to the solutions to today's problems with it. Naturally, I'd try to relate it to what we're studying in class." Greg waited, but Mr. Garsky said nothing. "I'll admit this means a lot to me personally, though. It bothers me to hear people whose friendships I once respected say they're prejudiced but that they don't know why. And the truth is, I don't have any other ideas for the paper. Not a single one. I tried hard to come up with one, but no luck."

"Excuse me for talking off the record, Greg, but do you really think that understanding prejudice eliminates it?"

"Well . . . yes. Yes, I do, Mr. Garsky. It's a first step, anyway. Don't . . . you think so?"

Mr. Garsky smiled. "Explaining something doesn't always explain it away."

"Well, I know it's hard. Naturally understanding a problem doesn't get rid of it overnight. I know it takes time."

"But how much time does a person have in a lifetime? Sometimes I think prejudice is an indelible mark." It almost seemed that Mr. Garsky had forgotten the reason for their appointment.

"Besides the fact that I ran myself short of time by waiting so long, I'm pretty busy these days," said Greg. "I'm not playing ball anymore, but I have a job."

"Oh, I didn't know that. Where do you work, Greg?"

"At a recreation center in Cole."

Mr. Garsky looked up suddenly; he seemed oddly surprised. "The one on Cole Avenue?" he asked.

"Yes, sir. I never had a chance to mention it, but I work with your niece Mitzi."

"Yes. Yes, of course you would. Good Lord, what a coincidence."

"She's a very nice person."

"Yes. She's very attractive. Have you ever met her fiancé?"

"No. But I imagine I will sometime. They say he comes around. He's a lucky guy."

"Yes. Tell me, Greg. Do you think you're prejudiced?"

Greg was surprised at the personal question. "No, sir," he said. "At least, I don't think so. I may have been . . . a little . . . before all this happened. But now, I don't think so. I feel everyone's the same, and that it's just a problem of ignorance. Anyway, that's what I'd like to find out."

"Well, good for you, Greg. Maybe you haven't been taught as strongly as some of us . . . as some of your friends and relatives."

"Maybe. My father is a social worker."

"Yes, that would help. Well. So much for that. 'The Roots of Prejudice.' Is that what you wanted to write about?"

"Yes, sir. Something like that."

"All right. The approach is a little unusual for our purposes, but there's no point in hashing over the fact that prejudice undermines our democratic workings. So you may make your investigation."

Greg smiled with relief. "Thanks a lot, Mr. Garsky."

"Now be careful, Greg. It's a bit different from the typical eleventh grade topic and you'll be working with a different type of material—psychology. So you'll have to keep it clean, clinical—if you know what I mean. No weeping, wailing or gnashing of teeth."

Greg laughed. "Don't worry. I'm past that point."

"Well, good luck. I hope you satisfy yourself."

"Thank you. I'll get started on it right away."

"Stop and see me after class tomorrow. I may have a book you can use."

"Oh . . . thanks."

On Sunday morning after breakfast, Greg ran upstairs to his room. Good, he thought. Light from the large east window poured over his desk just the way he liked. He sat down, fresh, eager, and pulled over some paper and a pen, and began scribbling down his thoughts.

After a short time, he examined Mr. Garsky's thick black psychology book, and as he read the relevant parts of it, the strange jargon of scientific discipline became familiar and human, for he had seen it dramatized before his mind's eye in the weeks past—a Negro being slandered because somebody had to be denied a job; a man despising the very body of a Negro because he had virulent attitudes about sex; a girl breaking up with her guy because he had a close Negro friend and embarrassed her; her mother, helping it along, because she wanted to be a member of a social group; a man saying that Negroes were inferior, so that exploiting them wouldn't seem so bad; the same man teaching his son prejudice, because he had to keep insisting that he was right; the son, a tragic product of learning and a twisted personality. All of them had been taught these attitudes; all of them were teaching each other; all of them were 'keeping in line'; all of them had to feel better than somebody else and were doing it the easy way; all of them denied inner guilt by projecting it onto the Negro. It was not like reading dull, dry facts; it was like seeing a puppet show. Mag Bryce rolled dead blue eyes while silly chatter emanated from stiff red lips. Thin, down-curved brows bobbed up and down over the dull grey eyes and painted distress of Mrs. Ashburn. A fat Toddy Johnson with jolly Santa's eyes and perpetually pursed lips boomed ho-ho-ho for the good boys and girls of Burnside. Henry in fixed weakness; Rich in fixed hatred; Virginia in fixed amicability—all filled out roles in the play.

It was a bright winter day. The light glaze of snow over everything glittered in the sunlight, and Greg squinted as he looked out the bus window at all the familiar landmarks on Cole Avenue. But today he was not getting off at Fisher Street. Today he rode past Fisher, past Jocusta where Jake lived, got off all the way down at Reed Street, and began the slow climb up the hill to his destination on Rydberg Street.

He had finished his paper quickly and turned it in, and now it was time to do something besides analyze people. He had been thinking a lot about Rich Wallace lately, of how Rich seemed bound up in his own little bubble by fears and frustrations that nobody else knew about. To them he was the pace-setter, the power figure whose favor they had to get to be safe. But to Greg now he seemed like a maddened animal, eating away at himself—always so red, so tense, so angry at something—and destroying those around him as well.

Power. It was such a serious-sounding word, a word reserved for the grown-up world, not the kind of word you would use for the petty intriguers of a middle-class high school. But pretty soon Rich would be out of high school and out of college, and what then? He would certainly be able to do more than scare a bunch of teen-age yokels and rally them against a couple of others. I am the only one who knows this, Greg thought to himself. And maybe it was time he stopped being the cool one, the superior one, the knowledgeable one. Maybe it was time he put his understanding to work, instead of using it to look down on others. To continue in that way was to be as guilty as the rest of them. Maybe even worse.

Crossing the color line, he knew, was still something remote in his experience. It was still something the extraordinary people did—the entertainers, the weird-oes, the people from the other side of his world. But if he ever ran across it in his own life, he would not, he felt now, really care. As for doing it himself—all right. So he wasn't ready. That didn't mean he was a hypocrite. It would take a long time, he knew, for all the things he had read in the past few weeks, all the things he had seen in the past months, to become part of him. And that wasn't the important thing, anyway. As long as he wasn't ready to "lynch the Negro," as Dad had put it, he was all right. And he knew he'd never feel that way.

He was finally up at Rydberg Street. He crossed over. It didn't look like much, the undistinguished purplish-brown building with Harris' Bar on the first floor—no different from every other building all the way down as far as he could see, and if he hadn't known this was the place from the address in the telephone directory, he'd never have even spotted the letters "NAACP" white-washed on the second floor windows. It was a start, anyway, he thought as he walked to the front of the building. At first he stood dumbly near the doorway to the bar while a groggy old man on a bar stool stared back at him; then he decided to check a side door he had seen. It was ajar, baring steep wooden steps and some printing on the wall:

HARRIS HALL
TO RENT FOR
WEDDINGS, BANQUETS, PARTIES

SEE SKINNY HARRIS, PROP.

Under it was taped a sign saying NAACP HEADQUARTERS, and an arrow pointed upwards.

The door at the top of the stairs was open and through it Greg saw a handful of teenagers. Three of them were white. He looked over the dingy hall, the small stage, the folding chairs. He hadn't even been sure any teenagers belonged, but the woman on the phone had told him that there was a junior division that met on Saturdays at two. One of the girls, a blonde with freckles and twinkly blue eyes, spotted him and came over.

"Can I help you?" she said.

"Yes. I'm looking for the NAACP, the teenage...."

"That's us," the girl said pleasantly. "Come on in." She had a big, grinny smile and made the dumpy, old-fashioned hall come alive. "My name's Pamela Trout," she said. "What's yours?"

"Greg Davis."

"Your first time here, Greg?"

"Yes. Yes it is." He felt self-conscious. It had seemed like such a big step for him, but this chick was so casual....

"I'll introduce you to some of the kids," she said. Among them was the junior chapter president, Sue Fowler, a slim colored girl with glasses. By the time they were done with the round of introductions more members had trickled in. "Well, Greg," said Pamela, "it looks like we're fighting a losing battle. You'll just have to make yourself at home. Do you live around here?"

"No," said Greg. "But I work at Cole Rec."

"Where?"

"Cole Rec. The recreation center a few blocks down."

"Oh yes. I've seen it. We may be doing some things down there."

"Aren't you from around here?"

"No. I'm from Aurora Heights."

"Oh. Do you go to Aurora High School?"

"No. The University High School."

"Oh." Greg wondered what had brought her here. But it would have been tactless to ask. And he'd probably sound stupid to these kids, he thought.

"You'll have to excuse me now," Pamela said. "I have to get things in order for the meeting." She walked away and sat down at an old wooden desk. Greg wondered if she was an officer.

There were about twenty boys and girls now, mostly colored. They didn't talk to him except to say hello. He wasn't sure what he had expected. When the old clock in the back of the hall said two, Sue Fowler called the meeting to order. Pamela, apparently the secretary, read the minutes of the last meeting. Then Sue spoke again. She talked about the efforts at Christmas employment that some of the colored high school students had made.

"Our senior committee on employment will follow it up," she concluded. "We're glad for the two who got jobs this year, but we're sorry that so many didn't. There's still a lot of work to be done, and we need more members to do it. I guess that will be the main business for the beginning of the new year—recruiting members and setting up new high school chapters. Our one experiment with them is a success. The one Pam and Marg and Jeff set up at the University High School has almost forty members already. But then, that's the University High School." Greg wondered what she meant. "You can begin by posting bulletins. Anybody have any more ideas about it?"

The crowd tossed the idea around for a while, then they talked about other things, like a drive they were having for toys and books for the orphanage. Marguerite James, one of the white girls, had arranged for her father, a sociology professor at Mansfield University, to give a talk sometime after the holidays on education and prejudice.

"Last but not least," Sue Fowler said, "is our annual Christmas get together. Skinny has a wedding here the Saturday before Christmas, so it'll have to be on the Saturday after Christmas. We're playing Santa Claus—fifty cents for members, but guests come free. And everyone is invited—I should say urged—to bring a guest. A new member. That's about it for today. Anyone want to make a motion. . . ."

"I move that the meeting be adjourned," said a boy in the front row.

"I second," mumbled his friend.

Everyone got up and a din of scraping chairs and murmuring filled the hall. Greg walked up to Pamela. "Do I register for membership with you?" he asked.

"I'm the gal."

"Well . . . here's my buck. I . . . uh . . . work every other Saturday, so I won't be here all the time. . . ."

"Uh-huh," Pamela said as she wrote his name, half anticipating and half believing what he was saying.

"Well . . . I'll be seeing you again . . . Pamela."

"Good. We're glad you came," she said.

Greg walked down the steps and looked up and down Reed Street. Well, what had he expected? People to run up and kiss him?

———⚊⚊———

"They were so casual and routine," Greg told his parents when he came home. "But to me it was surprising that kids . . . high school kids . . . would be interested in discrimination. I mean really interested. Interested enough to do something about it, to actually start chapters."

"Yes, I guess it would be for you, Greg, coming from such a different kind of community than the University High School is in."

"Yeah. That girl Sue made a remark to that effect. What did she mean?"

"Well, when you meet people with black skins, yellow skins, brown skins, Hindus, Moslems and Jews who have twice the brains and money as you, all that talk about superiorities and inferiorities starts to sound pretty hollow. That's the kind of atmosphere those kids are in. Take that James girl. Last year her father had a year's leave and he took his whole family to India. Now, a girl with that kind of experience is bound to be a little more broad-minded than someone with a more conventional background like Virginia."

"Boy. I'll say. I wish I could have gone to a school like that."

"Well, Greg, when we were buying a home, we weren't exactly thinking of your social conscience at the age of sixteen. And Burnside is an excellent school."

"I know. But these kids I met today. . . . they have guts. They know what's going on. My old gang is still going around in circles over stupid little things."

"Mah man!" Jake sang as he jogged down the steps for the Blackhawks' Tuesday practice session.

"He-ey. You're in an awfully good mood about something," said Greg.

"Things been happenin' since last I saw you."

"That was only last Friday."

"Yeah. But I got a call from some folks from Mansfield University on Saturday, and you know what?"

"Tell me all."

"They invited me to take a biology course up there next semester. What do you think of that?"

"Hmm. It must be the advanced standing program."

"What do you mean?"

"You take a course at the university and get college credit

for it. You miss gym, study hall, home room and lunch in one lump to get your time."

"How do you know so much about it?"

"Oh, it's been a regular practice for a couple of years already. I guess maybe they never had anybody from Cole who qualified for it."

"Guess not. Shoot! There's no telling you Burnside folks anything new, is there now?" Jake said, shaking his head. "You in that deal?"

"Not this year. I hope to do it in history next year, though. I know one girl who's taking chemistry now, and she was in the science fair last year. How's your exhibit coming along?"

"Aw, that's all done. Miss Hyde drove it down Saturday morning."

"And what's the latest on Little Red?"

"They're still pretty sure he's new on the scene. But they're still checking him out with some fancy science institutes. They're gonna make a special display of him at the fair, giving credit where credit is due, naturally," said Jake, playfully pompous.

"You're doing all right, Jake. Really getting up there. You can celebrate your new outlook on life by going to a party with me. The junior division of the NAACP in Cole is having a little shindig on the Saturday after Christmas. You've heard of the NAACP, I presume?"

"Yep. I used to think it was a lot of snow, but now I think maybe it isn't. Things have been turning out all right for me, so maybe there's a lot can be done for other people."

"Yes, there is."

"Where is this party?"

"Reed and Rydberg. A place called Harris Hall."

"Know where Skinny's Hall is, if that's what you mean."

"I guess it's the same place."

"All right. Sign me up."

"Do you know a girl named Sue Fowler? She's the president."

"Nope."

165

"She goes to your school. She's a senior."

"Guess I just know all the wrong people."

"And we can go to the fair, too. We'll stop there before the party. But we've gotta talk about it some other time. I've gotta be getting upstairs."

"Me too. Gotta work. We're gonna be starting the playoffs pretty soon."

"Yes, I see the Blackhawks are doing all right."

"Sure are. We're gonna come out on top. You wait."

As Greg gazed wearily out of the gym window the following Tuesday, the snow was falling thickly in the black night. He was sorry he had tried to act tough by sticking it out at Cole. He had had his doubts about going to work after school when he first felt the chills and the fever; now he knew he had made a mistake. Even Mac was out tonight. There was always a larger than normal number of absentees from school the last day before a big vacation like the Christmas one, but the even larger number today had been due to the serious flue epidemic. By last period Greg had begun to feel that stiffness, that watery blurriness of the eyes, that blending flux of heat and cold through his body. But he'd wanted to make those extra few dollars and wish everybody a Merry Christmas. He had figured he could shake it off.

But he hadn't. By six-thirty his eyes felt thick and heavy as though filled with glue; his body felt as though someone had poured moulten iron through a hole in his head. Then the fever flared up. And the sore throat. And the nausea.

The center was jammed with kids crazy with freedom and Christmas spirit and more demanding than ever. Scores of wild black children whirled around him as though pinned to an amusement park centrifugal rotor, while he, in the center, felt ready to throw up. The gym lights blazed in his eyes and the children's shrieks clamored in his ears. He almost resented them. They were so savagely happy and he so racked with pain. It was no use. He turned from the window and began walking across the gym floor.

And Mitzi and Doc. They had been pretty silly all evening, just because her boyfriend was home for the holidays and would be picking her up. To hear her giggling with Doc, you'd never think there was so much to do tonight. Little savages were probably downstairs tearing up the game room, and she was up here acting as though nothing was happening. He could hear her giggling above all the racket, as though she were hiding somewhere in his head and giggling just to needle him. Everything was a scream, a shout, and the fever was steadily getting worse.

He painfully bent down to pick up a basketball somebody had left in the corner near the office and he could hear her talking. "And then he said 'Some of my best friends are Negroes'", and she and Doc laughed. Greg wondered what was funny about that. One of his best friends was a Negro, too. He felt dizzy again. It was a heck of a way to start the Christmas vacation. Well, he was going home. If Mitzi had so much time on her hands, he thought, she could close up by herself.

Greg walked slowly to the office with the basketball and stopped by the desk. "It's no use, Doc. I know it's over an hour yet, but I feel lousy."

"Sure, Greg. We can manage. You should've left before, boy. I told you that."

"Poor Greg!" said Mitzi. "Go home and get some rest. I'll put Roy to work when he gets here."

"Thanks," Greg muttered. He dragged himself into the staff room, put away the basketball and went behind the screen to change clothes. But all he could do was sit in the wooden chair and stare. He thought of the snow that was falling outside. It was that thick, wet kind and he had no boots. Right now he wished he were conked out in bed, but he didn't even have the energy to get up and go home.

"There he is!" Doc suddenly shouted. "Welcome home, boy."

"Hello, Doc," someone strange said in a deep voice.

"Roy!" Mitzi squealed. "I was afraid you wouldn't make it in this storm."

Greg swore to himself. He clenched his fists and punched his thigh for having taken so long to leave. He certainly didn't feel like going through introductions and drumming up cordialities for the . . . big lover boy. They talked nonsense for an endless time; they would still be in the office.

"How's it going up at law school this year?" Doc asked.

"Fine, fine," answered the strange man.

Big deal, thought Greg. He started to dress. How would he ever make it home?

"Roy has a bigger fellowship for next term," Mitzi chirped.

So the man was a big deal at State. Greg buttoned his shirt and slipped on his shoes.

"Good, good," said Doc. "That always helps."

Greg zipped up his jacket, took a deep breath, and started out to the office.

"Greg!" Mitzi practically pounced on him. "I'd like you to meet my fiancé, Roy Harris." Greg turned. "Roy, this is our new junior counselor, Greg Davis."

Greg looked up and felt as though someone had suddenly slapped him awake. The sting was miraculously gone from his eyes; the cloud from his mind. Everything was clear again, unbelievably clear. But like a paralytic he was frozen and couldn't make a move. He tried hard but he couldn't seem to swallow the lump in his throat that was blocking that necessary, courteous first hello. He knew he was looking stupid and awkward, but still he couldn't say anything. He hoped that his eyes hadn't popped enough for them to see; he hoped that he hadn't stood there struck dumb for too long a time. But . . . why had they done this to him, springing it on him without any warning? Why hadn't anyone mentioned. . . . But why should they have?

He had been waiting far too long. Say something, he thought. Say something, stupid. And finally, with the careful weighted warmth and casualness that he knew he had to muster, Greg said, "How do you do?" to the tall Negro who stood before him.

"Hello, Greg," Roy Harris said with a warm smile.

"I . . . I was just leaving early. There's something going around, and it's hit me, too," Greg said, laughing nervously. "I . . . I'm sorry I have to run out like this, but I have a bus to catch. Well . . . Merry Christmas everyone." He smiled awkwardly and left, the good wishes of Doc and Mitzi and Roy Harris trailing after him.

That night in bed Greg was in full fever, and he saw thousands of humming charred masses collide and break in grotesque designs in his brain. He had acted like such a fool. And he had been such a fool about so many things.

He awoke a second time on Wednesday morning. It was the first day of Christmas vacation. The fever had subsided a little and his head was clearer now. Too clear. His first thought was that it was going to be a long Christmas vacation and he felt a little afraid. He had never spent it alone before. This Christmas he had no girl, no friends. Not even Jake . . . now. They were worlds apart. He knew that now.

He thought about last night. It had all been a big joke, this loafing around with Jake, going through all kinds of conflicts. But no, Jake didn't owe him anything. Jake had never asked him for anything, had never expected much from anyone. He had learned not to the hard way. He probably wouldn't even be surprised if he knew that last night his white buddy had rejected him like all the rest.

It was all so unfair. It seemed like a dirty trick of some mean agent in the universe who didn't like Greg Davis and wanted to humble him. Without even giving him a chance. After all he hadn't asked for this. It wasn't as though he'd wanted to make a Negro friend, knowing full well that he might have to pay some unpleasant penalities in the end. He had simply stumbled into the whole thing and played it by ear. And he had been the only one out of tune.

Once, when he saw that their friendship might cost him a few things, he was dumb enough to think it didn't matter, because he had his convictions, his independence, and most important, his honest affection for Jake. But last night had shown him those were all part of a big self-delusion. The test had come, and suddenly all the Negroes and crusaders and color-blind people could say, "Nice try, kid. But you just don't have the stuff." And he didn't even have a consolation prize. Sixteen years old and he had nobody.

He looked out the window. The snow had turned to drizzle and he was glad. Maybe it would keep some of the kids at home alone, as he was now. Otherwise, the kids would be out reveling in the holiday, the girls wearing fur hats and looking so pretty with rosy cheeks and snowflakes clinging to their hair. Greg shivered. He still felt weak. He pulled the covers over his head and sank down into the warm, protective womb of sleep.

Soft rapping on the door awakened him the third time. He sat up, startled, and called, "Who is it?"

"Dad."

"Come on in."

"We were getting worried about you," Greg's father said as he opened the door. "It's going on two."

"I've slept late before," said Greg, yawning. "I wouldn't care if I slept the rest of the day."

"No good?"

"No."

"Hmm. Then maybe you ought to stay in bed. You were really out when you came home yesterday."

"I was?"

"You looked awful. Your mother tried to make you something to eat and you growled at her."

"I was feeling pretty lousy. On top of that. . . . Dad. Something happened at the park yesterday. I . . . I'd like to talk about it."

"Well, why don't you have a hot lunch first?"

"It's a drag."

"I'll bring something up. We can still talk."

"Okay."

Greg lay down on the bed on his stomach and stared at his desk. His study lamp bowed and gawked over the side of it like some grotesque, coil-stemmed lily. Stupid-looking thing, Greg thought. That's how he must have looked last night he decided, as he stared at the yawning end of the conical shade—like a gaping mouth on the end of a scrawny neck. On the shelf near the lamp was a carbon copy of his paper for Mr. Garsky. Words now. Just words. At first he couldn't stand to touch it—but he finally did. He wanted to see what he had read about race. "Anthropologists know more about what race is not than about what it is," he had written. And he had gone on to tell what they knew it was not—that race wasn't a matter of blood, because everyone's blood was the same; that it wasn't a matter of traits because traits were learned, not inherited; that it wasn't a matter of mental or moral capacities; that it wasn't a matter of evolutionary level; that it wasn't even a matter of color, really, because so many Negroes passed as whites. The whole paper talked about nots—except why Roy was not like Mitzi. The whole paper, as had the thick book, talked about nothing, Greg thought bitterly. And he pushed it aside.

And as for himself. . . . Like some self-styled saint, he had been up there, wondering, judging, trying to understand and . . . casting stones. He, who was supposed to know better, wasn't without sin. And he, like the rest of them, didn't know why. Nor could anybody tell him why—why he couldn't bear to think about Roy and Mitzi . . . together.

Two raps on the door, and his father entered with a bowl of soup and a hamburger. He waited while Greg ate, then asked, "What's on your mind?"

"You know that girl who works at the park? Mitzi? The pretty one who goes to Mansfield University?"

"Yes?"

"She's engaged to a Negro."

"Well!" said Mr. Davis, surprised. "You don't run into something like that every day."

"How could she?" Greg demanded.

Mr. Davis looked at his son with a puzzled expression.

"Yes, that's what I mean. I didn't like it. I was shocked. It almost made me sick. And there's no use in trying to understand it any more."

"Is that what you wanted to talk about?"

"Talk, talk. Read, read. What good does it do?" Greg recalled Jake's words that one time so long ago. "You think you can make things work out just by putting the pieces together." Or reading about it, or thinking it out, Greg said to himself. "Explaining something doesn't always explain it away." Mr. Garsky had said that. "Once you're prejudiced, nothing's going to change it," Greg went on. "It's like a . . . spot in the eye. A stop sign. You look at a Negro and you say 'That's a Negro. He's off limits.' You can analyze and dissect all you want. Nothing's going to change it."

"What . . . am I supposed to say?" asked his father.

"Don't you see? All these things—I went to Jake's house; he came here; we went places together; worked on things together; I defended our friendship; we even fought together—none of them mean a thing now. After all that, I . . . I feel like I ought to just crawl in a hole and get out of everybody's way. Here I am, trying to straighten everyone out and I'm confused myself."

"Greg, you're not so bad."

"Oh, no. I don't seem so bad. That's the whole trouble. I'm a phony, that's what. People look at me and say, 'There goes Davis, the big crusader. He has a genuine Negro friend.' They don't know that deep inside Davis is the same as they are, that he's on their side when it comes down to brass tacks. When it comes to taking a Negro right into the heart of your life, into your family. When it comes to that."

"We talked about this before, about trying to decide what we'd do in hypothetical situations—what we'd do IF. It's

172

pointless. You've got to worry about doing the right thing now, and it seems to me that you have, Greg. . . ."

"No. That's not enough. You've got to *feel* it. That wasn't just Roy Harris standing there with Mitzi last night. It was all Negroes, including Jake."

"Surely you didn't hate that boy last night?"

"Hate? God, no. I hope I never hate anyone. But it was an awfully strong dislike. A distaste so strong that it bothered my conscience. And my common sense. I remember being afraid that I was staring and looking stupid, as though . . . as though I knew there was nothing wrong . . . except with me." Greg's eyes brightened. "Dad, I did know I was wrong."

"Of course. And wasn't that enough?"

"No. It's not. Not when you have a Negro friend. And not when you can't get rid of the feeling. Or even understand it. Dad . . . in all that reading I did for the paper, I didn't come across anything that explains why I felt the way I did."

"Well, these things are pretty subtle. Uncle Jack is right—you remember the talk we had on Thanksgiving—in saying that these explanations don't strike home. Somehow it seems that the psychologists and sociologists are talking about a different thing than what we feel in our hearts. But I told you what I think."

"That business about taste?"

"Uh-huh. Aesthetics, I'd rather call it."

"I don't know. Even if you were right about that aesthetics business, it would only explain why I wouldn't want to . . . date or . . . marry a Negro myself. It doesn't explain why I reacted to Roy Harris the way I did."

"You're attracted to this Mitzi, aren't you?"

"Mmm. You said it."

"Well suppose she were engaged to a good-looking white boy. How do you think you'd feel?"

"What do you mean?"

"Do you think you'd be jealous?"

"Aw, not really. I mean, she is four years older than me. She's not in my league anyway."

"Would you feel anything else?"

"No. What else is there?"

"All right. But suppose she were engaged to a severely ugly white boy. One that was deformed, perhaps."

Greg stared at his father.

"Don't try to analyze the question. And don't worry about sounding cruel."

Greg was shocked; then it was as though light flooded his head. That was it. It was the same kind of feeling. "With Mitzi?" he finally said. "It's . . . unthinkable. I . . . I wouldn't like it. I'd want to . . . pull her away. I . . . wouldn't want him to . . . to touch her." For the first time his feeling had been pinpointed and put into words, the pieces had been put together once more, and he felt released. He looked down, sad and ashamed of himself. "But this Harris," he said after thinking for a while, "he's what you'd call a good-looking Negro."

"Then you admit that you think some, perhaps most, Negroes are ugly?"

Greg flinched.

"Do you, Greg?"

"Oh, Dad. . . . why?"

"It's all what you're used to, Greg. And what you've been taught. All the cruel things you've heard people say about the Negro and how he looks and acts. Those feelings you read about, the things you've seen in other people exist in you, too, because they're the only attitudes you've ever known. It's hard to believe, I know. On top of that, you've never really known any Negroes before Jake. All you knew were stereotypes—stereotypes of stupid Negroes, ugly Negroes, dirty Negroes and vicious Negroes who stab people on the streets. And you're afraid, too. You're afraid of what other people think."

"Me? Afraid?" Greg said indignantly, thinking of his wilful alienation from the ties that had once been important to him.

"Greg . . . think hard. Right now, do you think you really want to lose your prejudice completely?"

And Greg did think hard, about so many strange possibilities. "I'm afraid to," he finally said. He nodded his head slowly. "Yes, I am afraid. I am afraid of thinking different."

There was a long silence as Greg and his father waited for the catharsis to spend itself—the man with compassion and sympathy; the boy with nausea and self-disgust. "God, it's so complicated," Greg finally said. "Will I ever change? Can anyone?"

"Stop worrying about getting rid of the feeling. Patience never was one of your stronger virtues," Mr. Davis said. "You couldn't push things no matter how hard you tried. You have to wait it out. But just keep on doing what you're doing. Learn. Hang on to Jake. Work for the NAACP. It takes time. But if it'll make you feel any better, I think you'll find some of that feeling gone after today." Mr. Davis rose. "I'm going downstairs to help your mother set the table for dinner. We're eating early today."

"Dad. . . ."

"Yes?"

"How do you know all this?"

Mr. Davis smiled. "Once upon a time there was a sixteen-year-old boy named Tom Davis." He winked and left the room.

Christmas Day. Not a white Christmas, but the people Greg saw as he leaned over the back of the couch and gazed out through the living room window didn't seem to mind too much. They seemed satisfied with the few lonely flurries that spun and swooped like ballerinas with whole stages to themselves and finally vanished. He thought of Virginia, and wondered what she was doing and whom she was going out

175

with tonight. Then he spotted two other girls in his class. Margie, a pretty blackhaired girl, had on a bright red coat, and Linda, a blonde, was dressed in black. They tottered as they walked down the street in high heels, but they both had nice legs. They were both chattering at once. No problems. For a moment he wished he had a date for the evening, but he wasn't crushed. He felt isolated, but not lonely; strange, but not sad. And a little older.

He was startled by the sudden shrill brrrring! of the telephone. His father had it right away. "Hello? . . . Oh, hello, Jake. . . . Merry Christmas to you, too. . . . What's that? . . . You did? Congratulations. That's a nice Christmas present, isn't it? . . . Yes, he's here. Hold the line."

Greg was already at the phone. "Hi, Jake."

"Merry Christmas," came a happy voice at the other end of the line.

"Merry Christmas to you, too."

"I called you yesterday early," said Jake, "but your dad said you weren't feeling so hot."

"Had a bug for a couple of days, but that's all. I'm just about over it now. Didja get my card?"

"Yeah. Thanks. I didn't even think of writing any. . . ."

"That's okay."

"Got a letter, too."

"Yeah?"

"Yep. 'Dear Mr. Williams, the Mansfield Science Fair committee is pleased to inform you that you have been awarded second prize in the collections division of the sixteenth annual science fair. . . .'"

"Great! Is that twenty-five bucks?"

"Uh-huh."

"What'd Aunt Sallie say?"

"Oh, she was funny, man. You shoulda seen her face. She said"—and Jake raised his voice to a shrill pitch—"Humph! I guess you think you pretty smaht!" The boys laughed.

"And your dad?"

176

"Aw, he was proud. Went down the street and told all the boys. I know 'cause I saw one of his buddies. And you know how my dad don't usually say anything."

"Well . . . Jeez, that's great, Jake. I'm pretty happy about it, too."

"Hey. You doin' anything this afternoon?"

"Yes. We're going over to my uncle's for a Christmas dinner. But I'll be home tonight."

"Hmm. No good. I'm invited to a party with some of the kids from school."

"The kids from school? Are you changing your social circles?"

"Yeah. I'm a good boy now. Ain't you goin' no . . . anywhere?"

"Uh . . . no."

"Got a chick for tonight?"

"Uh . . . no. I don't want to be running around after this flu, you know."

"Yeah, that's rough."

"I'm going to stay home and rest after we come back. Maybe I'll make out some New Year's resolutions. Yeah. That's what I'll do. Make out New Year's resolutions."

"Hmm. You're the hardest guy to catch. Guess I won't see you till Saturday then."

"Right. What's up?"

"You'll see. You gonna pick me up down on the corner?"

"Yes. Now I'm curious."

"Well you might as well forget it, because I ain't telling you a thing. Anyway, I've gotta knock it off now. So goodby. I'll see you Saturday. Down on the corner."

"Good-by, Jake. Tell everyone Merry Christmas."

New Year's resolutions. That was a good idea. It would make him look ahead instead of brooding over things past. He ran up to his room and took out some paper and a pen.

Jake was holding a big box when Greg met him on Saturday. It was gift wrapped. Greg pulled over to the curb. Jake opened the door, grinning broadly, set the box on the seat, pushed it over, and squeezed himself in. "Merry Christmas!" he said excitedly.

Greg looked at him with confusion on his face.

"For you," Jake said, jutting his chin out at the box.

"Jake!"

Jake chuckled with a silly self-satisfaction.

"Jake. I . . . I never expected. . . ." An impatient beep of a horn called Greg's attention to the green traffic signal. They started up. "Now what'd you go and do that for?"

"It's not much. And I wanted to thank you for all you've done for me."

"Aw, I never did anything special. And a simple thanks would've been enough."

"It's all right. You did a lot for me. And you've been through. . . ."

"Forget it."

"I know this is something you'll be able to use."

"It's big enough. What is it, a watchdog or something?"

"Open it. Pull around the corner. We're early enough for the museum." Jake was beside himself with excitement.

They parked and Greg began carefully slipping the red ribbon and silver paper off the cardboard box. Neither boy had a knife, so Jake helped him pull open the flaps of the sealed box. Greg lifted them and gasped with surprise.

"Holy . . . !" He looked up into Jake's shining brown eyes. "These must have cost you a fortune. Did . . . did you use up all your prize money? Aw, Jake. You shouldn't have. That's . . . that's a heck of a way to begin saving for college."

"Don't worry. I'm gonna keep working at it."

"Jeez, what a boob I am. I haven't even thanked you yet. These are the greatest. They're like . . . the gospel of the history world. I'll be able to use them practically all my life. Where did you find out about these books?"

"Just asked the man who knew the answers. Got one of the

history professors up at Mansfield on the phone and said, "Mah man, I know a cat who digs history. This boy's gonna go all the way to the top. And he likes to read. The high-class books, that's what ah'm talkin' about. The deep, deep stuff. Now, I'd like to lay some good history books on 'im because he's a good head. So whad'ya say, professor, do you have any suggestions? Put down mah finest words, of course, but I got the news."

Greg laughed and shook his head slowly. "This is very thoughtful of you, Jake. I'll never forget it."

Jake winked and signaled his approval with a wave of the hand. "Now we'd better get on with it," he said, "because it's a quarter to one. By the time you get a parking space and all."

"Jake . . . why don't you keep that microscope?"

"You tryin' to pay me for these books, Davis?" Jake piped.

"I know it sounds that way, my saying it now, but that's not the way I meant it. Honest. I've been thinking about it for a while. I even talked to my parents about it. About how you would really use it. Now . . . please take it. I'd be so happy if you did. I mean it, Jake."

"I think you do. Shake on it."

At the science fair Jake seemed to know a lot more about all of the exhibits than Greg did. "Been here before once. Did a little reading lately, too," was his explanation.

"Little Red," still without a biological name, was in his own showcase, conspicuously apart from the rest of the biology exhibits with a prominent legend.

A NEW DISCOVERY?

Entomologists at the Mansfield University Biological Research Institute seem to think so after extensive research and investigation. Discovered by Jacques Williams, a junior at Cole High School, it was brought to attention at the current science fair largely through the interest and efforts of Mr. Williams' biology teacher, Miss Jennifer Hyde.

Much of the information used in the study of the specimen was provided by the outstanding observation of Jacques Williams himself, who kept the beetle alive in a natural habitat during the summer of 1960 and took notes in an effort to find clues that would lead to its identification. Unfortunately, after this particular specimen died, no others were found.

Although Mr. Williams' notes are far from complete, they represent the kind of scientific observation and speculation which marks the kind of young scientist that this Fair seeks to discover and encourage. We commend Jacques Williams for what appears to be his original contribution to science. . . .

There followed some detail about Little Red. Greg shook Jake by the shoulder and said, "Hey. That's you they're talking about." Then they looked at the first prize exhibit in biology, which, as Jake pointed out, was a more comprehensive sample of the insect world. Then they went over and looked through the chemistry, physics and math exhibits.

"Shoot!" Jake said at one point. "Wish we had a decent chemistry teacher at Cole instead of that mess they laid on us. I just may want to do an exhibit in chemistry next year. . . ."

"Next year?" Greg looked at Jake and smiled.